Introduc

I first met Annmarie when I gave a story workshop in the *Carousel Creates* writing centre. The workshop focused on exploring memories and rediscovering incidents from your past that could become the seeds for fictional stories. It was about discovering the emotional heart of the incident and creating a fiction to illustrate that emotional kernel.

Many aspiring writers find it difficult to make the transition from memory to fiction. They do not trust the fact that, as a writer, you can embroider, distort, and reshape events and still remain true to the emotional truth. But Annmarie got it immediately. She discovered an incident from her childhood and whoosh... before you'd say hush to a duck she had made a new story from it.

Little did I know that day what was being unleashed on the world! In next to no time she was producing two blogs, *Fictitious Amo*, and *AuntyAmo.com*, which was nominated in the Personal Category of *Blog Awards Ireland*. Now she's produced her first collection of stories *The Long & The Short of it* and she only started writing these stories in September 2012. Even whirlwinds are jealous of her energy!

Annmarie's stories tell of people we all recognise, of people who, normally, are unsung and forgotten, of the mothers and fathers, the brothers and sisters, the neighbours and friends who live all around us – of people like us. She charts the trials and pains, the longings, the hopes, the disappointments, the tragedies and the everyday epiphanies of ordinary lives.

I can't wait to see how she develops.

Catherine Brophy

Author Bio

Born and raised in Tallaght, now living in Kilcullen, Co. Kildare, Annmarie Miles is a committed Christian married to Richard, a Welshman. Annmarie says she was "raised on songs and stories" in a musical and talkative family.

Annmarie's own writing, for many years was of the song persuasion. Instead of getting her mother's classic beauty, she says, she got her father's high forehead and ability to write a funny rhyme. It never occurred to her to try to write anything else…until now.

She started blogging in 2007 and says she used it to "think out loud" for a few years. In 2010 after being offered a regular column in *VOX Magazine* (and Irish print quarterly), Annmarie realised that it was time to take writing seriously. So she relaunched her blog as *Just another Christian woman… talking through her hat!* and began to interact with readers and writers on social media.

In 2012 something changed and it wasn't just that she turned 40. Annmarie realised she'd been bitten by the writing bug and decided to pursue the craft. After her first piece of fiction was completed there came another… and another, and since then the stories have flowed every day.

She continues to write her column for *VOX Magazine*, has a monthly column on the US website *Writer's Fun Zone* and has written a number of guest blog posts. In October 2013 her story series 'Lizzy,' which was written as part of a daily blogging challenge, began as a serialisation in *The Echo* newspaper.

Dedication

This book is dedicated to my 27 nieces and nephews.

Maria, Karen, Mark, Peter, Lyn, Emma, Brian,
Brenda, Susan K.A., Sarah, Jennifer F., Philip, Jean,
Dillon, Christopher S., Susan S., Claire, Laura,
Jennifer K., Christopher K., Katie, Kevin, Michael, Liza,
Beth, Jack and Bobby.

Kids, if I have any legacy to leave it will be going to you.
Chances are these stories will be it! Hope you like them.
I love you all very much, Aunty Amo x

To Fran

Sorry to miss you tonight.
There's a bit of Mellors
in here :).

Thanks,

James (Keeley) Miles

The Long &
The Short of it

By
Annmarie Miles

November 2013

The Long & The Short of it

2013

Published by Emu Ink Ltd
www.emuink.ie

© Annmarie Miles

Cover design by Gwen Taylour

ISBN: 978-1-909684-32-4

Acknowledgements

This is longer than some of the stories, but all are part of my story...

To you, the reader, the characters don't live because I've written them, they live because you read them. So thank you!

To Derrick Edge, the first person ever to say to me 'You're a good writer, you should do something about that.'

To my Twitter buddies who have encouraged me along the way and made 'virtual friendship' a tangible thing.

To the many writers I've encountered online, who have openly shared what they know and inspired me to press on, get better, be realistic and, no matter what, keep writing. Especially Ken Armstrong.

To my writing groups - *Kilcullen Writer's Group* and *Shared Planet Writer's Group*, for the coffee, chat and honesty.

To all the followers and readers of my two blogs *AuntyAmo. com* and *Fictitious Amo*, and my *#amowriting* Facebook page.

To Ruth Garvey-Williams, editor of *VOX Magazine*, for letting me find my voice.

To Jeff Goins for his generosity; and the *Tribe Writers* gang for bringing an online course to life.

To Carolann Copland at *Carousel Creates* who started off as a teacher and mentor but has become a dear friend; also the *Carousel Creates* gang, including Bernadette, Madeline, Annette and Fatima.

To Louise Phillips and Catherine Dunne - two authors who have read my stories and taken the time to give advice and encouragement.

To Catherine Brophy, another inspiring author who taught me how to write a story – thanks also for writing the introduction.

To Emer Cleary at *Emu Ink,* for chucking out the stories that would take from the book and recognising the ones that could sparkle, if I kept polishing! For the personal service and dedication to getting this book just right, and for making the self-publishing experience way too easy!

To my family
My Dad - who gives us all a story to tell.
My Mam - who gave us all a song to sing.
My brothers and sisters - for singing the stories with me over the years.

To my husband Richard
My beta reader and the maker of many meals when I've disappeared to write. This is only the beginning love, don't hang up your oven gloves just yet... I love you x

To God
Though you are not explicitly mentioned in this book, every redemptive moment, every opportunity for forgiveness and every glimpse of hope is inspired by your Good News!
LORD, unless you build this house, I am building it in vain.
(based on Psalm 127:1)

Contents

The American Wake

TEARS were rolling down Evelyn's face as she filled the kettle. She knew she only had a few minutes to gather herself before Peter would be down the stairs. After clicking the button she went back to the frying pan. It was bulging with sausages, rashers, white and black pudding. She'd ignored his protests that he could grab something at the airport. There was no way he was leaving this house without a good breakfast inside him and God only knew how long it would be before she'd get to cook for him again. With that thought, the lump in her throat swelled and she tried to roadblock the tears with her eyelids – but to no avail. His enthusiastic footsteps made her jump and dry her eyes quickly.

"Ah, Ma. You didn't have to do this... Can I have a fried egg?"

Peter kissed her on the cheek then sat at the table to check his paperwork for the tenth time. As Evelyn looked at him, memories of him sitting at that table over the years came flooding back.

The first day he'd sat there instead of in his high chair, barely able to see over the table. He managed to cover it, and himself, with bits of carrot and mince from his bowl of stew, but Evelyn didn't care.

The Christmas Day he got the mini snooker table – they'd had to eat with their plates on their knees for about six weeks afterwards; he refused to move it. But it was the best present he'd ever had and he still talked about it. He never knew that Evelyn had borrowed from a money lender – it was the first Christmas after Peter's Dad had left them and she was determined he'd have what he asked for.

He had sat at the table struggling with his maths homework in primary school and again when he was in secondary school. He was always terrible with numbers

3

and there were tears of frustration when he tried to study for the exams.

Sitting in exactly the same place, he had opened the letter confirming the job offer in Boston six weeks previously and Evelyn had cried that day too.

"Ma, MA, my egg will go hard!"

Evelyn turned back to the cooker and took up the breakfast. Peter made tea and they sat at the table.

'One last time,' she thought to herself.

"What time is your taxi booked for?"

"Plenty of time. Another couple of hours yet. Are you sure you don't want to come? You can just get another one back."

"Ah no love, you go on. Sure I'd be like an eejit trying to find a taxi after you're gone."

"You'll have to come and see me. When I get my own place. I'll probably have to stay with Jack for a while, but when I have me own apartment you can come."

They chatted away for another half hour, making plans that would never come to pass and promises that would be impossible to keep.

A ring on the doorbell made them both jump.

"Your taxi is very early. He better not charge you."

"He won't charge me!" Peter was determined as he walked to the door.

Evelyn knew immediately that it was not the taxi driver and started to clear the table, presuming it was one of his mates coming for a last goodbye. After a minute or two, however, the voices at the door grew louder and she could sense that it was not a positive conversation.

Evelyn peeked out the kitchen door and saw a man who was vaguely familiar. A wave of recognition swept over her and she dropped what she had in her hand. The noise made Peter run to her and the visitor followed him.

The next thing she knew she was on the sofa and Peter and his Dad were standing in front of her, arguing.

"Stop, stop it. Just stop it." Evelyn stood up and the men fell silent.

"Martin, what do you want? What are you doing here? You're not welcome."

"I just came to say goodbye to my son. I won't stay and I wouldn't still be here if you hadn't made such a fuss."

Peter was about to jump to Evelyn's defence, but she stopped him.

She looked at her husband for the first time in more than 10 years. He was thin and gaunt, like someone who had been living on the street and had borrowed a bigger man's clothes for the visit.

"I just wanted to wish my boy well. I've been keeping an eye on you over the years Peter and I heard you were heading off today. I just didn't want to miss my chance to... to say goodbye."

"Your son? Your boy? I haven't been your boy since I was nine. If you've been keeping an eye on me you've been doing a crap job. The only one who's been keeping an eye on me is Ma."

"I don't want to cause trouble. I'm not staying, I just wanted to say goodbye." As he said the words he looked as if he was going to faint. Instinctively Peter and Evelyn grabbed him and led him to a seat.

"I'll get you some water." Evelyn walked to the sink and Peter followed her.

"I'm not going." Peter was speaking in urgent whispers. "I'm not leaving you with that mad man. I don't even know if it *is* me Da. He could be some nutter."

"He is your Da; and you are getting on that plane if I have put you in a taxi and take you to the airport myself. You are not wasting five minutes of your life on him."

5

Evelyn gave Martin a drink of water.

"Do you want some tea? There's a bit of fry there if you're hungry." Evelyn's default position – when in doubt feed somebody.

"No I'm grand, I'll have my water and go. I'm sorry. I didn't mean to cause trouble."

"My taxi will be here soon and I'm not getting into it 'til you're gone out of this house."

"Once I've had my drink I'll be gone son."

"DON'T call me that."

After a few minutes the doorbell rang again. They all stood in the garden until the tut-tutting of the taxi driver eventually encouraged Peter to put his bags in the boot. He hugged Evelyn for what seemed like an eternity, but it was not long enough for her and she lost the battle with her tears again.

"I don't want to go 'til he's gone Ma."

"Get into that taxi or I'll box your ears."

They laughed and cried and then they laughed again.

Peter turned to get into the taxi and stopped. Evelyn had brought him up too well to turn his back on Martin, no matter how much he hated him, so he put his hand out and Martin grabbed it.

"Thank you. Thank you, Peter. Goodbye and good luck."

"I don't want to hear you were at this door again."

"I won't be, I promise."

Another long hug for his Ma then Peter was in the taxi and gone.

Evelyn and Martin watched their son's taxi drive away until it completely disappeared, then they stood for another few minutes; motionless and silent.

Without looking at him, Evelyn spoke to Martin. "How long have you got?"

"Six months maybe. The doctors reckon it could be more if I sort myself out a bit."

"Can I do anything?"

"No. You've already done everything Evelyn. He's a grand young fella."

Martin started to walk away.

"I can help, let me help." Evelyn couldn't stop herself.

"I made a promise to that lad and for once I'm going to keep it. Goodbye Evelyn. I'm so sorry."

Evelyn watched Martin walk away and as her heart broke for her son, she was shocked to find that there was room in it to break for Martin too.

She mourned them both for a very long time – her saving grace knowing that at least one of them would be back.

Neighbourhood Watch

RODDY McCarthy's front garden could hardly be seen through the sliver that once was the gated gap in the hedge. The gate disappeared behind the greenery, which was overgrown in every direction. The grass looked like it had never been cut and the pathway to the door was more like a trail through the undergrowth.

The kids on the street would often throw a ball in his garden and dare each other to retrieve it. Once, when a bike was thrown over Roddy's hedge, the poor kid who owned it was too afraid to get it back and too afraid to tell his mother. After two weeks, and a clip around the ear from his father, he eventually braved Roddy's garden.

Most of the time Roddy didn't even realise the kids were in and out of his garden, but every so often they'd strike gold and make his dog Smithwicks bark. Roddy would then come to the door swearing like a trooper, promising all sorts of dismemberment and disfigurement to the kids that he considered, "no better than bloody pond life," for ruining his day.

Nobody knew where Roddy had come from or if he had any family. He'd been there longer than anyone on the road and all that was left was rumour and counter-rumour. There may or may not have been a wife. Some say she died and others that she left him because he was a drinker. Old Mrs Muckerty was convinced he had killed her and buried her in the garden, but her sister, even older Mrs McDonagh, insisted that it was only because she didn't like him. He had promised to take her to a dance half a century previous, but took someone else instead. They, along with all of Roddy's neighbours of that generation, were now gone and the mystery was left in the hands of a new set of families. Some were children and grandchildren of the old guard and though Roddy's garden was still good for the odd game of 'chicken', none were really interested in the answers to those questions.

Raymond and Anthony Maher, or Mondo and Anto as they preferred to be called, were the bravest of all the lads on the road. One Saturday evening they decided that they were going to ring the bell and knock on the door at the same time. That would drive Smithwicks mad and they figured they'd be well gone before Roddy got to the door. They spread the word so they'd have a good audience – there was no point doing it if there was no one watching. A gang of kids from the road jostled for position either side of Roddy's gate as the Maher twins set off on their stealth mission. There were comments, laughs and shushes from the gate but the twins were focused as they crept up the pathway.

Anto got ready to press the bell as Mondo lifted the heavy brass knocker, and he was about to give the signal when the door suddenly opened. Mondo dropped the knocker and it banged louder than anything he'd ever heard. He looked for Anto but he was already running up the path to the shouts and laughs of the audience. Mondo froze for a second then realised he was face to face with Roddy. Before he could move Roddy grabbed him, pulled him in the door and slammed it shut.

When Anto got to the gate everyone ran to the safety of Brady's shed, six doors up from Roddy's. Only when they were inside with the door shut did they notice that Mondo wasn't with them.

"Where's me brother?" cried Anto panic-stricken. "WHERE'S MONDO?"

*****

The first thing that hit Mondo was the smell. It was like a combination of old cigarettes, damp dog and petrol. He thought he was going to be sick and had to work hard to keep it down. Roddy had let go of him as he tossed him into the corner. Mondo was surprised at the old man's strength and as he landed he half expected a kicking, so he closed his eyes tightly. The only thing he felt though was Smithwicks' rotten breath on his face. Underneath the sound of the dog's breathing was a quiet steady growl. Mondo dared to open one eye. He'd never realised that Smithwicks was such an ugly dog.

Roddy was sitting in a chair nearby, catching his breath. Mondo opened his other eye and knew immediately that Roddy had got a bigger fright than he had. He knew he had the upper hand but stayed where he was. He wasn't as sure of himself where Smithwicks was concerned.

"What were you doing at me door?" Roddy looked like he'd had the stuffing knocked out of him and was secretly relieved that Mondo hadn't thrown a punch at him.

Mondo answered Roddy but never took his eyes off Smithwicks. "Eh, we were eh, just, you know, calling in to eh, see how you are."

Roddy laughed so hard he gave himself a fit of coughing and had to take another minute to catch his breath.

"See how I am? Well now, that's the first time anyone on this road has been bothered about me for over 30 years." Roddy wasn't laughing anymore. His face and tone changed very quickly with bitterness.

*****

Back in Brady's shed Anto was trying to get someone to tell him what they saw but they were all talking at once. Except for Teresa Brady, she was crying and was louder than the rest of them put together. Anto let a roar and everything went quiet. He then asked them to tell him, one by one, what they saw. Each of them said the same. The door opened, a hand came out, grabbed Mondo and then he disappeared. Anto was relieved that none of them said anything about his running away with the fright; but they all thought it and they would always look at Anto Maher a bit differently from now on.

Michelle Ryan put her arm around Anto to the tuts and groans of the other boys. "Don't worry Anto, he'll be grand. I bet you anything he'll be back here in five minutes." Anto shook her arm from his shoulder, he hated when she did that in front of everyone.

"Well if he isn't here in five minutes, we'll have to go back for him!"

They sat, listening for the sound of Mondo coming up the path but all they could hear was Teresa Brady, still sniffling.

*****

"I've had enough of you kids." Roddy was up off the chair. "I said when I saw that young eejit getting his bike out of the garden that the next time I caught yis there'd be trouble. So I'm ringing the Gardaí. Fed up I am, fed up to the back teeth. No privacy in this house. How high does that hedge have to grow before I'll be left alone? And poor Smithwicks, driven mad with the noise of you lot out on the road. Can't get a moment's peace around here. Well I've had enough. What you did was against the law so that's it now. Do you hear me? That's it."

Mondo was so relieved. The police would do nothing. Roddy was just an oul' mad man and he'd had them out a few times. If Mondo could just get out the door, he knew they'd all be in Brady's shed waiting for him. As Roddy ranted on, Mondo was imagining how brave everyone must have thought he was. He reckoned with a bit of luck too Michelle Ryan might now prefer him to Anto. And didn't Anto leg it off on him? Chicken! Mondo realised he'd probably emerge very well from all this…

Roddy, now addressing him directly, stole him from his thoughts.

"Well? Well? Answer me! I asked you a question at least have the decency to answer me. What's your name, 'til I ring the guards?"

"Can I go if I tell you my name?"

"Yes!" Roddy was eager for him to be gone anyway.

"OK, I'll tell you then." This was Mondo's favourite bit about being a twin…

*****

It was more like 15 minutes before Anto and co. decided to walk towards Roddy's house. Anto said that he thought the girls should stay with Teresa as they didn't need anyone whinging, but they all wanted to go and he eventually gave in.

They walked slowly down the road, looking at each other but saying nothing, and just as they got to Roddy's gate, Mondo appeared. There was a squeal of delight from the girls and calls to 'shut up' from the boys as they all ran back to Brady's shed. They let Mondo get his breath back. Teresa Brady was crying again and was shouted at by nearly everyone to be quiet so that Mondo could tell the story of his capture. They looked at him in awe and he rose to the occasion.

"I thought he was going to cut me head off." Mondo had them in the palm of his hand – well, everyone except Anto. He knew Mondo better than anyone and was dividing the story by half as he listened.

"Smithwicks went for me. He's a mad dog – like a little wolf! He had me boot in his jaws and I had to shake him off. Roddy was shouting, 'Kill Smithwicks, kill.' Mondo acted out how the dog almost ate him, but he managed to fend him off. The eyes of the girls got wider and wider, and the lads were more than impressed.

"Were you not afraid of your life Mondo?" Michelle gazed at him as she spoke and Anto was starting to get annoyed.

"Roddy is a mean oul' mad man, but I wasn't afraid – he knew he'd met his match."

Anto had heard enough. "Right Mondo come on, we have to go home. See yiz all tomorrow right?" Mondo got slaps on the back from the lads, smiles from the girls, an emotional hug from Teresa Brady and even a wink from Michelle Ryan. This was a good day.

The twins walked home in silence but just before they got to their own gate Anto turned to his brother and said, "Sorry for legging it Mondo. I really thought you were behind me. If I'd'a known he grabbed you I never would've ran off. Sorry bud." He offered Mondo his hand.

"No probs bud, but you owe me one alright?"

They both laughed and shook hands.

"Yeah alright, I owe you one."

*****

A few days later, the Gardaí arrived at the twins' front door. Their mother brought the officers into the sitting room where Anto, Mondo and their Dad were watching telly. Mr Maher looked at the men and then looked at his sons.

"How can I help you?"

"Mr Maher, we've had a complaint from Roddy

McCarthy about your son."

"That oul' eejit? Sure he hardly knows what day of the week it is! What did he say?"

"Well he claims he had a full conversation with your son after he tried to break into his house."

Mr Maher looked at his sons again. Anto was cool as a cucumber but Mondo was stunned. He never expected Roddy to go through with his threat.

The Garda continued. "So we're going to ask you to come to the station for an interview. You and..." He checked his notebook. "Yes, your son Anthony."

"WHA?" Anto shot a look at Mondo, who was now carefully examining his feet.

As Mr Maher tried to reason with the officers about the innocence of his son, Mondo shrugged at Anto and whispered, "Sorry bud – but we're even now yeah?"

The Matchmaker

AS Angela scanned the queue, her instincts drew her to Mary; maybe she was the one. Did she need love in her life? Angela had been looking for 'the one' for quite some time. She was very confident in her sixth sense and mystical insights, even though they had yet to prove fruitful. Undeterred, Angela believed that when instincts arose in her, the answer was always close.

A kerfuffle drew everyone's attention as a man almost fell in the door, tripping over a woman trying to get out with her shopping and a tribe of small children. Everyone watched him apologise profusely without actually getting out of the woman's way. She ploughed passed him regardless, kids in tow, and was out of sight long before he realised he was now apologising to the post office door.

Angela was surprised and delighted to see Mary leave the queue and walk over to him.

"Ray? Ray Nolan is that you?"

Ray squinted at Mary, then his face lit up.

"Mary Walker, I don't believe it! How are you? I haven't seen you since I don't know when."

Ray stuck his head out the door and shouted, "Sorry about that" to the long gone woman and her kids. Then he let go of the door just as a little old lady was about to go through it. After more apologising, Mary and Ray walked to the back of the queue.

Angela was so impressed with herself. She was getting very good at this and now it seemed her mere presence in a room could spark a connection.

She listened to them catch up and talk about such-a-body who was married with triplets and such-a-body who'd moved to the US and was now working in the White House. They laughed about old school photos that had turned up on Facebook and discussed the never confirmed rumour that Mrs Roache, the art teacher, had

had a fling with Mr Kenny, the maths teacher.

All the way up the queue they reminisced. Angela could hardly contain herself and hoped she'd hear at least a swapping of phone numbers before long.

Then she heard the words she was waiting for…

"So, what about yourself Ray? Are you married?"

"No, no. Haven't met the right girl yet. Mammy says it's cos there's only one or two good enough for me."

Angela smiled.

"Awwhhhh. How is your mammy?"

"Not a bother on her. I'm supposed to be meeting her here actually. So you might get a chance to say hello. And what about yourself Mary?"

Angela held her breath…

"Oh yeah, married four years – ah here he is now."

Angela could have cried as she watched the tall, handsome man come through the door.

"Mary, I got stamps in the newsagent's hun." Ray's rival called over to her.

There was a brief introduction and all too soon Mary and her champion were gone.

Ray then spotted Angela.

"Oh hiya, Ma, didn't see you there. Did you see Mary Walker? That was her and her husband. D'you know, Ma, I must be the only one out of my class not married or gone abroad?"

Angela looked at heaven, then at the floor and finally, with a loud exhale at Ray said, "Yes love, I do know."

A Life Saved

MERYL stood at Jem's bedroom door. He was a newborn the last time she felt this helpless as a mother. She could hear the weird music. He was watching those old horror sci-fi movies again. It wasn't a good sign. The eerie wailing had worried her when she'd heard it first, but she eventually recognised the sound of a Theremin, that instrument so adept at falsifying an atmosphere of mystery and impending doom.

It didn't need falsifying today.

It had been three days since she'd seen him. He hadn't come out of his room to eat or use the bathroom, or if he did she wasn't aware. The only reason Jem's Dad, Tom, hadn't broken the door down is that, eventually, Jem would answer their pleas for response with a grunt to be left alone.

Meryl knew he was drowning in guilt; she was devastated for him and felt powerless to help him.

It wasn't his fault.

It wasn't anyone's fault.

Jem and Carl often spent their time exploring old Jennings' farm. They'd learned to fish in his river, he let them pick apples in his orchard and every so often he'd pay them to paint or clear the yard. He was a bit of a loner but the boys never caused him any trouble and he liked them.

It had all gone wrong though, when the boys did the one thing he'd asked them never to do. They couldn't see his truck in the yard and thought he was out, so they climbed the frame of the dilapidated wooden water tower. When Jennings saw them from a distance it never occurred to him that it was Jem and Carl. He got his shotgun and started firing in their direction. He didn't want to hit them; he just wanted to scare them to get them down.

It worked. Carl got such a fright he almost let go, but

Jem grabbed him and pulled him up. The beam he caught hold of, however, gave way and Jem watched Carl fall to the ground.

At Carl's funeral Jem read a goodbye letter to his best friend. It was a heart-wrenching elegy of friendship, regret, anger and guilt. He had not spoken to anyone since.

That was two weeks ago and now he was locked away in his room. It was beginning to feel as if both boys had died that day. Meryl had a sense that somewhere over her head there was a battle raging for her son and she was determined she would win it. This filled her with strength, and power surged through her veins as she knocked at the door again.

"Jem, it's Mom. Please open this door – right now." Meryl was not going to walk away until he opened it.

Inside his bedroom, Jem was frozen in time. Any effort to console him sent pain racing through his body. He was so angry, with himself, with Jennings, with Carl, with everyone. The noise of the TV was supposed to be a distraction, but all it did was cause his mind to tumble and spiral as he relived the moment that Carl fell, again and again. The little sleep he got was disturbed with dreams; peace refused to come. He listened to his mother's voice coming through the door, simultaneously hating her and longing for her to hold him, like she did when he was a little boy.

"Jem I love you. Dad loves you. And Carl loved you; he would not want you to do this to yourself. Let your tribute to him be life, not more death."

"She's right you know."

Jem cried out at the sight of Carl standing in front of him. Meryl heard the cry and ran to get Tom.

"You have to live for us both now mate." Carl beamed

his goofy grin.

"I don't think I can. I don't know how to." Jem's voice was barely a whisper.

"Yeah you do. You get up every morning and do everything we were going to do. Jennings has more painting he wants doing and you need the cash for that stupid bike you're going to buy."

Jem laughed and the release of emotion was followed by a noise from inside him that became a howl of despair. He slid to the floor and cried out how sorry he was. He did not even hear his father burst through the door.

Meryl ran to Jem and gathered him in her arms. She rocked him for what felt like hours as he sobbed and apologised to Carl, every so often pointing to where he was standing.

Eventually he was still and sleeping in his mother's arms, like a baby again.

Tom sat on the floor beside Meryl and gestured an offer to take Jem, but she shook her head.

"What was he pointing at Meryl?"

"I don't know, but it doesn't matter now. I think he's coming back to us."

"I hope so love, I really hope so."

"He is," said Carl as he left the room – but neither of them heard him.

A Technical Hitch

THE question was making its way around the classroom and Maisie Dalton was getting more and more agitated. This was the kind she really hated and it got her the most grief in school; but Miss Pervis was new and insisted on knowing more about her pupils. Maisie was trying to work out how to answer the question truthfully without actually answering it, when her turn came.

"OK, who's next? Daisie Malton?"

The other girls went into fits of hysterical giggles.

"It's Maisie, Miss. Maisie Dalton."

"OK, OK girls settle down. Maisie, I'm sorry. So tell me, what do your parents do for a living?"

The room went quiet and Maisie cleared her throat. "Well it's just me and my mom and she, well she makes stuff and... fixes stuff."

"Ohh that's interesting. Is your mother a carpenter... or a mechanic?"

"No, not really, she is... well she designs things and makes them. She is... she's an inventor."

"She's a nutty professor!" Karen James shouted out. Maisie turned to tell her to shut up, but Miss Pervis was quicker.

"No one shouted out while you were speaking Karen, so please show the same courtesy."

Karen sunk back in her chair and turned a nice shade of pink – Maisie couldn't have asked for more, but she knew it wasn't over.

"Maisie that is fascinating," Miss Pervis continued. "Maybe someday we'll get you to tell us more, but for now we need to move on."

'I'd rather not, thanks', Maisie thought to herself as she shot a cutting look at Karen before the next person answered the question. Karen drew a circle with her finger at the side of her head, which made Maisie furious.

31

She turned to face the front of the class and didn't hear the answers anyone else gave.

When the bell rang Maisie managed to get out of the classroom and out of the school without talking to anyone, or hearing their comments. She would have loved to challenge Karen James and hit her for mocking her mom; but the truth was that she was afraid of Karen and knew it made more sense to keep away from her.

On her bicycle she made her way out of town and on to the road home. It was a long cycle but she didn't mind. When the weather was good it was the most beautiful place in the world. In the winter her mom would often collect her as there were no buses that went near where she lived, but unless the weather was really bad Maisie would insist on walking or cycling. Partly because she loved to be outside, but also because her mom actually did look a bit like a mad professor and the beaten up classic car did nothing to help. None of the other pupils realised how cool it actually was, all they saw was a crazy woman in an old car – but Maisie knew different.

At home she let herself in and kicked off her shoes. The downstairs of their house was one giant room with an open spiral staircase leading to the bedrooms. It was an old house and Maisie's mom, Patsy, and her dad Cuthbert Dalton III, who had been many years older than Patsy, had refurbished it all themselves. They knocked down walls, fitted a giant range where the old fireplace used to be, took away the old straight stairs and built the wood and wrought iron spiral staircase. They practically knocked the whole of one side of the house down too, but it was the side that faced the valley. Bert, as he preferred to be called, rebuilt it, fitting a large diamond-shaped window. For more than a year there was scaffolding around the house and even some on the inside, which pretty much held everything up while he worked on that one wall. But the finished product was a breathtaking view of the valley, whatever the weather, and each time she looked out there now she thought of her dad.

Maisie ran upstairs to change into some old clothes and when she came back down she spotted a note on the table from her mom.

'*In the workshop Maisie, snack in the fridge, Mom X*'

Maisie poured a glass of milk and sat at the table to eat her sandwich. She looked up at the range to the picture of her parents. Maisie had just started school when Bert died so she didn't remember him very well, but Patsy spent hours telling her about him, so she felt like she'd known him for a lot longer. She wasn't sure if you could *miss* someone you had so little time with, but she felt like she did.

Maisie was happy though and never happier than when she was at home in her modern and eco-friendly surroundings. Every mod con that had been invented, and one or two that were still to be patented, were on hand to make life that little bit easier. The house was powered and heated by solar and wind energy. Their hot water came up from an industrial well so deep in the ground that it was hot when it got to the surface. Their Wi-Fi router was the size of a matchbox, it was a prototype that only a handful of people in the country were testing and it was 50 times faster than any service available. There was a whole stock of smaller gadgets that her mom played around with, tried for a while and then did some more work on, including everything from cameras to icemakers and printers to toasters. Maisie's favourite gadget was in her own room. It was a telescope built into the ceiling. When she pressed a button, a panel in the roof moved like the sunroof of a car and opened up to a whole new world. The eyepiece and focuser were by her bed and she often fell asleep while looking at the stars.

When she'd finished her snack she went out to the workshop. From the outside it looked like a big old corrugated iron outhouse. It was a deliberate ploy so as not to excite any interest into what might be inside. Maisie strained to open the large heavy door.

She loved the workshop; to her it was a wonderland. Her mom kept it perfect. The inside walls were panelled wood and there were racks, shelves and lines of nails for stuff to hang from. She had boxes and boxes of papers with designs and drawings of possible machines and contraptions that she, or Bert, had tried their hands at over the years.

Every so often Patsy would dig through one of them to find the plans for a small device she'd thought of years previous, that had then proven the answer to a problem for another invention. There was a workbench that stretched the full length of the workshop along one wall, with every tool you could imagine and quite a few you couldn't. If Patsy didn't have the tool she needed she would invent it and make it. The woman was a genius. Not many people, not even Maisie, knew that she and Bert had worked for NASA for many years; it was where they had met. They weren't astronauts or even brilliant physicists but they could solve any problem and make any device that came into their heads. Some of the cleverest people in the world came to them with problems and they worked out how to solve them. If the piece of kit didn't exist to fix it, they'd make it.

After Maisie's dad died Patsy left her job to be at home with her daughter. NASA begged her to stay and offered everything they could think of to help her, but in the end they reluctantly let her go. They still commissioned her privately, however, to do some work for them. It turned out to be a perfect solution. Patsy would never need a 9 to 5 job to support herself and Maisie. She could be at home with her as long as Maisie needed her but she could also get to work on some of the more 'down-to-earth' inventions that were rolling around her mind.

Inside the workshop there was no sign of her mom, but Maisie loved to wander around. She knew better than to touch anything, she just loved to look at all the tools and half-built gadgets. There was a notepad and a pen, which every so often contained Patsy's scribblings concerning each thing she was working on, but Maisie had no idea what any of it meant.

'Too much power needed. Smaller structure perhaps?'

'Back to square one!'

'Will need to be password protected.'

'Wooden frame too dense – metal instead?'

Her mom's voice came from above her head. "Amazing Maisie! Hiya honey."

"Mom you made me jump! What are you doing up there?"

"I was out on the roof, checking the solar panels. Got a reading that one of them wasn't working properly so I was checking it out." As she spoke, Patsy was climbing down the metal frame that doubled as a shelving unit and built-in ladder to the roof.

"So," she said, jumping the last step to the ground. "How is my Maisie huh? Did you learn lots today? Are your neurons firing, making all sorts of cool new connections? Huh? Well? Did something fall into place today and make you go… AHA!" At this she did another jump and pointed at the sky with both hands.

Maisie laughed at her. She always said that learning new

stuff was one of the greatest things that could happen to anyone.

"Actually Mom, remember I told you we've a new teacher? She wanted to know all about us and who we are and what our…." Maisie didn't want to go there. "Anyway, the teacher was doing the learning today. Although I think she's struggling to remember everyone's name. It's just her second day."

"Well now. Here's something interesting about that…" Patsy went into a technical description of how the brain works connecting names and faces. Maisie, as always, was a captive audience to her mom as she taught her in twenty minutes, more than she would learn that whole week in school. For a while, she forgot about Karen James too and all the other annoying things about school. She loved the idea that as her mother spoke, there were neurons firing in both their heads.

****

Back in school the next day, all the talk was about the upcoming musical. It was of no interest to Maisie, and the only reason she liked it was because it distracted Karen and her gang so they left everyone else alone. Although there were a number of teachers involved, and it would be directed by Mr Morrison, most of the production, stage-building and management was to be taken care of by the pupils. This was an area that Maisie might have been interested in, but the team seemed to be all boys; led by Ryan Abram. She really liked Ryan, and so avoided him as much as she could.

At lunchtime there was a big discussion and while Maisie was at the next table she could get the gist of what was going on. The Principal, Mrs Davenport, was retiring at the end of the school year. The last night of the musical was going to include a surprise presentation for her and the production team needed a way of working it in to the finale. Maisie was getting interested because the issue was a technical one. How would they get a cake, or a sign, on to the stage without the principal seeing it? How would they reveal it at the right moment? Ryan was surrounded by his stage crew and, of course, a number of girls, including Karen. As they discussed the problem, lots of suggestions were made but he was rejecting each one out loud, and Maisie was doing the same in her head.

Ryan hushed them all. "Look guys, we can get everything on to the stage easily as long as it is covered. The trick will be to uncover it in one move."

"How about a sheet? Then someone can pull it off as part of a dance routine."

"Danny you can't put a sheet over a cake, you doofas!"

"You could keep it in the tin."

There were a number of shouts for Danny 'not to be so dumb.'

"Hey maybe we should have one of those big cakes and have a stripper jump out of it." Everyone laughed at this, even Mr Morrison who had come over to listen in and see how they were doing.

"That's it." Maisie was on her feet and everyone looked around.

"That's it," she repeated. "Whoever is doing the presentation comes on stage hidden in a box then pops out holding the cake or flowers or whatever. The box will look like a prop; there just needs to be room for someone to hide in it."

"That's a great idea, you're Maisie aren't you?" Ryan looked impressed. Karen did not.

"Yeah," Maisie could feel herself blushing but kept

going. "It could be left on the stage or pushed on at the right time. "

"What about the sign though?"

All eyes were on Maisie and she was on a roll.

"Well, let's paint in on fabric and not wood. It can be rolled up and tied to something up high. If there's a long string and you tie it loose, one tug and the whole thing will unravel, then there's your sign." Maisie was wide-eyed and energised. Every face was smiling back at her, except Karen's but she didn't care.

"Maisie that's excellent." Mr Morrison was delighted. "Would you like to help? Be on the stage crew maybe?" A couple of the guys made faces but Ryan seemed really enthusiastic about the suggestion, so they said nothing.

"Yeah, I'd love that." Maisie was overjoyed.

****

She hurried home from school that day and told her mom all about it. Over dinner and throughout the evening they came up with all sorts of suggestions of how the box would work. They could even build a little seat in it so that the person holding the gift could sit down. The only problem Mr Morrison had seen was that if it was a big wooden box and had a person in it, it might be hard to push around the stage but Patsy and Maisie decided it should be on wheels, like casters and therefore easy to move. It was way past Maisie's bedtime when they finished talking about it but she wasn't tired.

****

At the first production meeting the main topic of

conversation was the box. It was decided that there were so many things to do, that Ryan and Maisie should work on that and the rest of the team should get on with other things. Maisie mentioned some of the suggestions that her mom had made and Ryan was amazed at how many great ideas they'd come up with. He had heard some crazy things about Maisie and her mom, most of them from Karen; but Maisie Dalton was turning out to be way cooler than any girl he'd ever met.

****

It was the last night of the show and Maisie's mom said she would come to see it as she had helped Maisie add an extra kick to the impact that the box was going to have. Instead of arranging someone to open a door in the box, Patsy had made a remote control device that would make the four walls of the box collapse. Maisie and Ryan decided not to tell anyone so that it would be a surprise to everyone, not just Mrs Davenport.

All week the reports of a fantastic show had made their way around town and there was not one ticket left for the last night. News had spread that there was going to be some acknowledgement of Mrs Davenport's retirement, so she was extra done up that night, fully prepared to be invited up on to the stage and photographed by local press. Maisie's main job was to make sure that Molly Black, the youngest member of the cast, was in the box by five minutes to curtain call. They'd decided that a cake was too complicated to have her hold in the box, so she had a large bunch of flowers. The outside of the box was painted in similar colours to the set so that when it appeared on stage it would blend in. The juniors had made the sign as part of their art class project and it was loosely tied to some of the rigging above the stage with a long string. Everything was ready.

Just before the second half was about to start, Ryan and Maisie went into to the crew room to get everything they needed, when they found Karen James looking at stuff on one of the tech tables.

"What are you doing in here? Only crew are meant to be in here." Ryan didn't sound very annoyed.

"I was just hoping you'd wish me luck Ryan, for my last finale number." Karen swished past Maisie and stood in front of him. Maisie thought she looked stunning. Her hair and make-up were done and her dress was like something from a Broadway show.

"Good luck." Ryan said eventually, once he'd got his breath back. He whistled as Karen walked out and Maisie felt a lump in her throat. She looked down at herself. She was all in black, which was the stage crew uniform. Her hair was scraped back in a tidy ponytail to keep it out of her way and she'd never worn make-up in her life – but that had never bothered her until now.

They got their stuff and went to take their places backstage.

The second half went great. The audience were singing and clapping and everything was all set for a finale that would be talked about forever. Molly Black was in the box, ready. One of the stagehands was posted by the rope to let the banner down and was told not to move under pain of death. Maisie had marked an area on the stage that no one was to be standing in for the finale. It meant moving a few people in the closing number but she promised Ms Scacchi, the choreographer, that it would be worth it.

"Hey, thanks for all your help Maisie. The show would

not have been this good without you." Ryan said as the finale was in full swing.

"Awh no, and anyway it's been great to be involved."

Ryan leaned over and kissed her on the cheek.

Maisie's world stopped for a moment. No one had ever kissed her like that. She stood as if she was paralysed for at least a minute and then she heard Ryan's voice again.

"Maze, Maisie, press the button. Maisie, the button."

Maisie jumped. She grabbed the small remote control in her hand and pressed the button. Nothing happened. She pressed it madly again. Nothing. The cast knew that if the box didn't open they were just to stay in their positions until Mr Morrison directed them otherwise. Maisie was pressing the button and sweating profusely – what was wrong?! Ryan grabbed it off her and shook it. "Did you put new batteries in it?"

"Yes!" Maisie was frantic, "just before the show started."

Ryan took the back off the control. There were no batteries in it now. They looked at each other and both said in unison, "Karen!"

Suddenly there was a crashing sound; the four sides of the box collapsed. As they did, they tore the seals that were set in each corner, which caused a serious of small explosions of confetti and paper string. Molly Black stepped to the front of the stage as Mr Morrison escorted Mrs Davenport on from the wings. The banner fell from the rigging to reveal the hand-painted sign from the juniors, on behalf of everyone, and the audience was on its feet.

Ryan and Maisie looked at each other, both shaking their heads and saying, "How did…? What the….?"

Mr Morrison, with obvious relief, gave Ryan and Maisie the thumbs up and they made the same sign back at him, still not sure what had happened. The only one who didn't seem to be enjoying the finale was Karen James.

Eventually Maisie's mom made her way back stage. "Fantastic, fabulous. What a show. WHAT A SHOW!" Maisie gave her a big hug and was about to tell her about the batteries when Ryan came over. "Mrs Dalton, thank you for all your help. Maisie told me that a lot of our tricks were your ideas. And the box… I've no idea what happened. I still don't know how it opened, did she tell you the batteries were taken out of the remote?"

"She didn't but now I get why there was a big pause and I had to put plan B into action." Patsy grinned.

"Plan B?" Ryan and Maisie said it together.

Patsy took a second remote control out of her pocket. "YOU?"

"Yep. It occurred to me today that there might have been some interference with the radio mic and other sound and vision equipment. You guys didn't want that moment to go wrong, so I thought it might be handy to have a second remote. I couldn't find you before the show so I had it ready, and boy am I glad I did? Looks like there was some interference huh?"

"Oh yes," Ryan said. "There was interference alright."

Patsy went home and allowed Maisie to stay for the afterparty as long as Ryan promised that she would get home safe. Karen James was seemingly taken ill just after the finale and had gone home too. Everyone had a great time and the crew was congratulated, along with the cast, on a fantastic show. Maisie was particularly popular with everyone.

Eventually people started to leave and Ryan and Maisie headed for the door, then Maisie stopped.

"How did she know?"

"Huh?"

"How did Karen know about the remote control? We

didn't tell anyone."

"Oh yeah, well ... I um... I kinda told her. We're sort of... well we *were* sort of... dating."

"Oh."

"Not anymore though. I can't believe she would do that."

"Maybe it wasn't her." Maisie couldn't believe she was defending Karen James.

"Nahh it was her alright. She was really angry that you were involved and that we were spending so much time together."

"Well she doesn't have to worry about that now. The show's over."

"What I do is nothing to do with her anymore; and anyway, I think we should spend more time together."

"Really?"

"Yeah, really – Christmas show prep starts as soon as we're back in September you know?"

They both laughed and Maisie pushed him playfully. In one move, he pushed her back and put his arm around her shoulder.

"Come on," he said. "I promised your mom you'd get home safe."

Change Of Scenery

MACKIE stood soaking up the breathtaking view that he loved so much. He leaned on his staff and surveyed the mountains. Every shade of green, and quite a few of brown, mapped out the view in front of him. In the far distance there were some angry-looking clouds, thick and black. Around the edges of them, grey and white clouds tried to dilute the mass of darkness but with little success. Where Mackie stood, however, the sky was blue with just the odd splash of white candyfloss above him.

He checked his car was locked and began his walk, breathing a sigh of relief. He did not know what he would do without his Sunday walk. It allowed him to shake off the stress of the past week and build his strength and energy for the one to come. Monday to Friday, and very often on a Saturday, Mackie was in a three-piece suit. His day started at 5am and if he was home before 9pm it was a short one. In his business it was non-stop work, eating on the run and drinking numerous cups of coffee. He was glad he never took up smoking; his colleagues who did were on their way to some serious health problems, if they weren't there already.

During the week he was Roland Mackintosh – Businessman, lawyer, cut-throat negotiator, demanding boss and trusted colleague. Mr Mackintosh to most; Roland, only to the equity partners. His presence in a room changed the atmosphere completely. There was no time for pleasantries or badinage. Roland Mackintosh was the reason that there was no 'dress-down Friday' anymore. As far as he was concerned if you weren't dressed for work, you weren't working. He would have cancelled the Christmas party and the annual team building day, but for the first and only time, he was outvoted in a meeting. Middle management described, in grave detail, the terrifying consequences of plummeting staff morale to all the other partners and the decision was made. Despite all that though, he was a loyal boss and defended his staff and their jobs – just not their perks.

On Sunday though, he was who he was meant to be – Mackie, nature lover, a man with few cares and an empty road ahead of him.

And here he was again, but today he was trying hard not to let Roland Mackintosh interfere even though he knew he would have to go into the office later for an emergency meeting. It was written into his contract that he didn't work on Sundays; a throwback to growing up the son of a Methodist minister, but he had no interest in that life these days. Still, a work-free Sunday was more sacred to him than any of his childhood religion had been. This, however, was a crucial meeting that he would have to attend. The jobs of many beneath him hung in the balance and he would not let mass redundancies happen without a fight.

It occurred to him that this was the first time he had contemplated work issues while on his Sunday trek and it felt a bit strange. Usually when working things out he would finger the chain of his father's old pocket watch, which was always in the pocket of his waistcoat. Then when he came to a conclusion, in one move he would throw the watch, quickly catch it and pop it back in the pocket. He actually missed having it with him.

As he walked he pondered the difficult discussions that would be made later. He didn't have a photographic memory but he remembered numbers; and numbers were the problem. The board felt that there were too many staff, the salary bill was too high, there was not enough customers and not enough 'billable hours' from the customers they had. Roland Mackintosh could rhyme it all off from memory. He also knew the numbers within the expense accounts and this is where he believed the real problem lay – Lavish dinners, trips abroad, top-of-the-range company cars that sat in the underground garage all day. Not to mention the numerous items marked 'sundries', which included expensive jewellery, villa redecoration and many unlabelled items, all of which resulted in large costs. Roland was determined that if the board insisted on a reduction in staff numbers, he was going to insist on a reduction in the expense accounts.

He made a mental note to ask Carla to take word-for-word minutes of the meeting. Carla had been Roland's executive assistant for 15 years. She came with him when he moved companies and there was no one he trusted more. She had put the meeting in his diary, and he didn't ask her if she could attend. It never occurred to him to do so; if he was in the office then Carla would be in the office too.

Mackie had never thought about Carla, not once. She was part of Roland's world and had no place in his Sunday life. He stopped and looked around again, and for the first time since he had known her, he wondered where she was and what she was doing. What did SHE do with her Sundays?

After a few moments, he shook his head to rid his mind of the thought and continued his walk, trying again to put anything associated with work out of his mind until the last minute. He breathed deeply as he took the lonely road and, as usual, was only passed by one or two vehicles in the hour that he spent creating a distance between himself and his BMW.

As he turned to make his way back he spotted another walker coming towards him. It was rare to find anyone else walking these roads. When they met the man asked Mackie if he had seen any sheep. Mackie laughed and said he had but far in the distance and spread across a wide area. It was what the farmer had feared. His Land Rover had a flat tyre and the jolt of the sudden stop caused the rickety back gate of his animal trailer to fly open and the sheep started to wander. The first thing that needed to be done was to change the tyre and he needed help. Mackie was happy to be of service.

"Art, by the way. Arthur Sandall."

"I'm Mackie. Pleased to meet you."

The two men shook hands and Mackie noticed his pale, manicured, moisturised skin against the rough, weathered, grimy hands of the farmer – but their handshake was equally firm.

"I've seen you up here before," Art said as they made their way towards the farmer's lame vehicle.

"Really?"

"Yes, I've passed you a few times on the road; usually I don't have to stop to rescue sheep. You must love it up here?

"I do actually, it's my therapy."

They both laughed.

"I see land and all I see is work."

"And all I see is relief from it."

They walked on is silence.

"Do you own much of this land?" Mackie asked.

"Quite a bit of it, but most of it isn't worth much. There'll be no fancy apartments built up here."

"Well there's no fancy apartments being built anywhere at the moment."

"True."

"So what would make it less work?" Mackie's interest in Art and his work was increasing.

"Well I had to let both my farm hands go so I'm running it all on my own and if my wife wasn't such a great administrator, as well as all the other million things she does, I'd spend all my days doing paperwork."

"Well the changes in landowner registration will have tripled it I suppose. And of course all the livestock have to be traceable now. Do you deal with FA directly or do you use one of those new agent services they're trialling here?"

Art stopped, obviously surprised at the stranger's knowledge and Mackie laughed.

"Sorry, I'm in law – not agricultural, but I keep up to date."

"Well you've just summed up our other big problem at the moment. We're struggling to get our head around these new requirements. If you don't mind me saying, you don't look like a lawyer."

"Well, I look like a lawyer from Monday to Saturday."

They reached the Land Rover and between them managed to change the tyre within a few minutes, after which Art was ready to set off in search of his sheep.

"Thanks for your help Mackie, I'd still be walking if I hadn't met you."

"Maybe I can help some more? Why don't you give me your number, I can look into some of the legal stuff and maybe simplify it for you so that it doesn't take up so much time."

"I can't afford a lawyer."

"As long as you're happy to talk on a Sunday, I'm happy to help."

They swapped numbers and Mackie turned to walk towards his car knowing he was a lot later than he'd planned. He rushed back and as he came down from the mountain he hit traffic that felt more like Monday morning rush hour than Sunday afternoon. It seemed there was a large event that people were spilling out of and quickly Mackie realised he would not have time to go home and change into Roland Mackintosh's three-piece suit.

He arrived at the office with only minutes to spare. When he came through the door Carla stood up and asked the bedraggled-looking stranger if she could help in any way. She then recognised him and struggled to hide her shock.

"Sorry, Carla I got delayed, then stuck in traffic. Is my other suit still here?"

"No, sorry, Mr Mackintosh." Carla couldn't take her eyes of him. "No, I'm sorry sir; it went to the dry cleaners on Friday."

"That's fine. Can you get me my notes please and tell the board I'll be with them in five minutes? I just need to get my head together."

"Of course sir." Carla left the room, still in shock.

As he waited he stood looking through the wall of glass out on to the amazing vista that his top floor office supplied. He rarely stood at the window and never took in what was out there; and so for the first time he realised that his office faced the same mountains that he had just descended. There were buildings in the way and they were a lot further off, but he recognised the distinctive shape of the mountain range; and just as Roland Mackintosh had been to the mountain for the first time, Mackie was now in his office for the first time.

Carla came back in with water, coffee and his folder of notes for the meeting. "Thank you Carla and thanks for coming in today. I really appreciate it. I hope I haven't ruined your plans."

Carla was taken aback; he had never said anything like that before. But she had had no plans. She would have been working from home anyway. Sorting files, replying to emails, booking accommodation for his next trip. His job was her life too.

The board could not hide their surprise when he walked in and he again explained the problem and apologised. The meeting started but Mackie found it hard to stay focused and looked out the wall of glass that faced the same direction as his own office. The mountains were calling to him and he did not want to be in this meeting.

"Roland? Roland, are you with us?"

"Sorry, Howard. Yes I am."

"So, what I'm saying is, Roland that these expenses are worked into staff contracts and it would take too much time and money to negotiate a major change. The quickest and easiest way is to reduce the staff numbers. We need to lose at least four juniors. Two at secretary level and two at trainee level."

Mackie looked out the window again, then back at the board members.

"What if I left?" He smiled as he spoke.

Everyone looked up, Carla stopped typing.

"I'm sorry, Roland?"

"If I leave the company, could the juniors stay? You can promote one of them and give them a raise instead of showing them the door. My salary and bonuses would more than cover the salaries of the four you want to lose. I'll go; I'll take the basic pension and no redundancy pay. Keep the juniors, and train them to be great seniors. I don't want to be here anymore."

"Where do you want to be?" Carla's voice came from across the room. In her distress she had forgotten herself and thought out loud.

"Out there." Mackie was back standing at the window, looking at the mountains. "I want to be out there."

He walked back to his own office, leaving the partners gasping in his wake, and took his keys and coat before heading for the lift. Carla met him in the foyer. She couldn't hide the fact that she was angry; she had devoted the last 15 years of her life to him and now he was just going to walk away.

"I'm sorry, Carla. Your job is safe here; I made sure of that when they drew up your contract. You'll be assigned to another lawyer, hopefully one that lets you have a life, but no matter who you're assigned to make sure you insist on *having* a life. I apologise for not allowing you that, but rest assured that this is a good move for you too."

It took him less than an hour to get back to the mountain. He parked the car and started his walk for the second time that day, just in time to see Art gathering some sheep into the trailer.

"Is that all of them?"

"I wish. What are you doing back up here?"

"Thought I'd come back and help you out."

"I already told you, I can't afford a lawyer."

"I'm not a lawyer anymore, now come on, let's find the rest of those sheep."

Singing The Blues

JOHN, Joe and Liam were inseparable; and if ever there was trouble you could guarantee that they were somewhere nearby. They whistled at every young wan, jeered every fella, criticised every footballer, politician and basically anyone who'd ever made a few quid. If there was no one around and they had nothing better to do, they slagged each other. None of them had a girlfriend but they weren't bothered. They knew the only reason they were all single was because they were way too cool for the local women. And anyway, a girlfriend would be breaking the oath that they had sworn when they were teenagers; more than twenty years previously; *'De Boys before De Birds – always'*.

Despite the lack of love in their lives they still had certain women who adored them – well most of them. John's mother, Bridget, thought he was the most wonderful son a mother could have. She *was* bothered that he didn't have a girlfriend, but tried not to let it get to her. John had her wrapped around his little finger and she ignored her daughter's regular, "you're worse" comments whenever John got his own way. To Bridget, John was a perfect example of all that a son should be. As far as she was concerned (even though most of these things weren't actually true) he was clever, good-looking, respectful and a hard worker who always went to Mass, yes... John was a good boy. The only complaint she had about him was the company he kept. As far as she was concerned, a bigger pair of gobshites than Liam and Joe there had never been in Ireland before.

Liam's mother had a completely different view. She thought that Joe was the shining star of the bunch. Joe was a couple of years younger than Liam and John and he had actually got to the stage of leaving home and getting his own place – something John and Liam had not quite managed yet. Liam's mother knew exactly what he and John were like and had no time for their "dossin' and wafflin'." She had a soft spot for Joe as he was younger and had "made something of himself." What she didn't know was that Joe had not actually moved out. He'd been thrown out, by his father, for bringing the police to the door twice in one month. Somehow, by the skin of his teeth he had kept his job and managed to get a little bedsit not far from the where the other two lads lived.

One Friday night the lads were in the local, knocking back the pints and eyeing up the girls. It was a week until payday so they didn't have much, but as usual whatever they had, they shared. John didn't hand up much money to his ma because, as she said herself… "God love him" (whatever that meant). Most of Joe's wages went on rent, so although he had the best job he was always the one with the least money and Liam's wages weren't bad but he gave a fair chunk of it up to his mother. She made sure if he insisted on living at home, he was going to pay his way. Although she'd have gladly gone without the extra few quid if she could just get rid of him – chance would be a fine thing.

In the corner of the pub some fella was setting up speakers. "Who's on Harry?" John shouted over to the barman.

"Kev the Karaoke King," Harry shouted back. "New thing now on a Friday. Bit of a competition…are you up for it?"

"I am in me…"

"Howya John." Sylvia Byrne smiled at John as she swished past the lads.

"Gowan Jonno ya good thing." Joe and Liam gave him at least 10 minutes of grief over Sylvia and he pretended to hate it.

"Maybe you should sing her a karaoke song. And IIIIII-eeeeee-IIIIIIIII will always love yooooouuu-eeeee-ooooo..." Liam gave the worst Whitney Houston impression ever known to man.

"Wha? Karaoke? Are ya mad? John can't sing."

"Shurrup Joe. Yeah I can. Remember at your ma's 60th? I brought the house down with me Wild Rover."

"Yeah and I brought me dinner up," Liam said into his glass as John punched his arm.

"There's no way you're going to win that," said Joe. "You'll only make a show of yourself."

They sat back in silence and then Kev the Karaoke King started to sing 'Pretty Woman'.

"Are you telling me I couldn't do better than him?" John was sulking now.

"If you were 10 times better than him you'd still be rubbish." Joe's comment made Liam spit beer all over the place and the two of them nearly fell off their stools laughing.

John wasn't giving up. "Remember that time we went to Wexford… we did a mean Blues Brothers in the car on the way down."

"Ahh will you shurrup we're not doing the bleedin' thing."

"OK ladies and gents. Remember, cash prize of €50 and three free pints to the winner," Kev the Karaoke King said, in his faux American accent.

Joe's conversion was a swift one. "Hang on! Wha? FIFTY EURO. Right, Blues Brothers it is."

"Wha? No way! Are ye mad?"

"Liamo there's fifty notes in it AND three free pints! Come on, John is right. That was a great version of Blues Brothers we did in the car that time." Joe was already

59

filling in one of the entry forms that had been left on the bar.

The karaoke competition got under way with Martin Murphy singing 'I can't help falling in love with you.'

"Wiiiiiiise meeeeennnn saaaayyeeeeee...." Martin warbled the first line as the girls screamed and the lads booed. He eventually got to the end and bowed as if he'd just won The X Factor. The three lads were in hysterics at the bar as Martin fell off the platform and knocked over the mic stand before landing on someone's table and spilling their drinks all over the floor.

"Elvis has wrecked the building." Liam shouted, and the three of them were hysterical again.

Next up was Gwyneth Jenkins. She was Welsh, so only Tom Jones would do. She sang Delilah and everyone was shouting the chorus with her. Everyone except Joe, who took exception to "a bird singing a bloke's song."

The three lads were called up next and the slagging was something wild. Sylvia Byrne was up the front of the crowd shimmying in front of John and screaming like a teenager at a Beatles concert. The lads blathered their way through the intro forgetting the words but when the singing started everyone was well impressed. All three of them had good strong voices and could hold a tune.

Joe sang the main tune with John and Liam doing echoing and filling in with "oohh oohhhs". They even had the little Blues Brothers run going. Although it did make the mics shake and even the karaoke machine table was jumping about a bit, so Kev gave them the nod to tone it down. When they were finished there were shouts for more and they were high-fived and back-slapped all the way back to their seats.

For over an hour Kev the Karaoke King called out the names that had been given to him. Some ran and grabbed the mic like their lives depended on it, others had to be cheered or even dragged on to the stage. One name was called out 10 times and Kev's accent got more Irish and less American the more irritated he got waiting for the person to respond. He wasn't a bit impressed to find that 'Nelly Nonote' was a fictional character made up for someone's amusement – certainly not his. He threw the daggers at the three lads at the bar who were avoiding eye contact while trying to keep a straight face.

When Kev's accent was restored he said, in an ominous tone, "OK guys n' dolls...." The room went quiet with anticipation. The sweat was pouring out of him as he got back on stage. "We have one more act for you tonight. Can you give a big welcome to our last contestant... the lovely, the B. E. A. utiful SYLVIA BYYYYYRNE."

Sylvia stood up to the shouts, whoops and whistles of the crowd and Joe and Liam were digging John in the ribs. Sylvia waited for things to quieten down and then gave Kev the nod. The whistling continued through the introduction to the Titanic theme tune, then the room fell silent as Sylvia belted out a heart-stopping version of the Celine Dion classic. When she finished there was a moment of silence as the crowd, with jaws dropped, savoured the last note. From the bar John's voice started the cheer and the applause erupted. Everyone stood up for a full five minutes; shouting, whistling and clapping; and Sylvia, embarrassed but delighted, blew coy kisses to the room.

There was no doubt who the first prize was going to and Kev the Karaoke King crowned his queen to more shouts and whistles.

When everything calmed down, the lads turned back to face the bar, their glasses and their pockets were empty as they momentarily begrudged Sylvia her win. Without a word they put on their jackets and were about to leave when Harry put three pints in front of them.

"Sylvia wanted to share her winnings with you lads," he said, before rushing to serve someone else.

Delighted, the lads took their jackets back off and turned to wave at Sylvia, who was surrounded by other fellas and couldn't see them. John picked up his drink. "I'll go over and say thanks to her for us lads," he said and disappeared into the crowd.

Joe and Liam turned back to face the bar.

"Do you reckon we'll see him again tonight?"

"Ahh yeah, he'll be back in a while."

But they didn't see him again that night, or the next night, or the night after that. And very soon John's mother got her two wishes as he made some changes to the company he kept.

Oxygen Deprived

"HAPPY birthday love." Maura's voice filled the room.

Ross opened one eye to see his mother standing by his bedside holding a large envelope with a big blue bow on it.

"Thanks, Ma. Do you mind if I open it later? I really don't feel very well."

"Ahhh, Ross I'm looking forward to you opening it because I know you're going to love iiiit."

Maura sang the last bit the way she used to when trying to get him to eat his dinner.

Ross opened his other eye and struggled to sit up properly.

Maura presented the envelope to him with a flourish. She had a crazed smile and was nodding enthusiastically – her eyes popping out of her head with excitement.

Ross peeled the envelope open with as much energy as he could muster. The card had footballs and cars on the front – neither of which interested him. When he opened it though, a smaller envelope fell out and written on it was:

'Ticket for collection x 1 – Murphy'

Now he was awake.

He shot the question to her with a look.

"Yes love, your Dad told me you asked to borrow the money and he wouldn't lend it to you. But I got around him."

"Ahh, Ma, I can't believe it – how did you even know what to buy?"

"Sure you've talked about nothing but that Oxygen thing at the racecourse for ages so I checked the googleweb and found it." She beamed, ecstatic that she'd pleased him so much. Ross jumped up out of the bed and hugged her neck until she had to push him away to breathe.

Then he pulled the ticket out of the envelope and his

face dropped and went pale. Maura's face dropped too. "What's wrong love?"

"This is… Ma where did you…?"

He looked at her. Her eyes were glassy with the promise of tears.

"Nothing, really I just don't feel well. Thanks Ma, this is brilliant. Thanks a million."

Maura left the room, relieved and delighted with herself. He could hear her as she went down the stairs, "Con, CON, what did I tell you? He's thrilled."

Ross let himself fall forward and flopped on to the bed.

He looked at the ticket again that read:

Join us for a fabulous day of world-class horse racing at the Oxigen Environmental Stakes, The Curragh Racecourse – Admits One.

His festival hopes dashed for yet another year.

Love Bubbles

ROGER the bubble floated through the air. In the distance he could see Barb. He'd liked her from the moment the two of them were blown out of the circle three seconds previously and he decided not to waste any more time. He turned in her direction and made his way towards her.

"Barb, Barb? You got a minute?"

"Sure Roger." She came towards him.

Roger decided that actions would speak louder than words and was all set to pucker up when he saw Clive.

Barb however, didn't see Clive and bumped straight into him, bursting Roger's bubble.

Corned Beef Sandwiches
On Brown Bread

MONA wrestled her way on to the bus. Two shopping bags were in each hand, her purse under her chin and her hat just about to fall off her head. "I have a pass love," she said as she tried to smile without dropping the purse. With barely a nod the driver closed the doors. Mona had just about enough time to steady herself before the bus lurched forward as she made her way down the aisle.

Ruarí saw her getting on the bus and almost got up to help her, but changed his mind; he wasn't in the humour of being thanked for twenty minutes. He felt a pang though as he saw her struggling with her belongings, but went back to looking out the window anyway. As Mona got closer and closer he was thinking, 'NO, NO don't sit here please!'

He looked up and she caught his eye. Mona stopped, smiled and said, "Can I get in there beside you love?"

"Sure," said Ruarí, and without missing a beat he tucked himself in to the window as far as he could.

"Oh, thanks very much. I'll be glad to get home for a cup of tea." Mona was squishing her bags in under her seat and the one in front. She put her handbag on her lap and fixed her hat.

Ruarí braced himself, now resigned to the fact that he'd have to talk, or at the very least listen, all the way home. He recognised her; he'd seen her nearly every day since he'd moved into his little bedsit across from her house. She reminded him a bit of his granny with her walk and her weird hats. He couldn't relax now, waiting for the chatter to start. But Mona said nothing as the bus moved along and now Ruarí felt uncomfortable. He presumed she lived alone. He'd never seen anyone go in or out. There was that pang again.

"Out doing your shopping?" He thought it sounded

lame.

"Oh, no. Well yes! But no actually. I was out shopping... but not for myself."

Ruarí was ready to be sorry he'd asked, but Mona left it at that.

He stared out the window again. His thoughts went back to the musings he'd been having before Mona got on the bus. How much he hated the dole office. How much he hated the dole officer! He was a bit worried about the scene he'd caused last week when he was there. He had lost his temper and started shouting and banging the horrible glass partition. Then he'd emptied everything out of his pockets and shoved it through the little slot, screaming that she could have everything he possessed if that was what she wanted. She then called for security and got him thrown out.

He had totally lost it and wouldn't have gone back today except that they wouldn't pay his rent allowance if he didn't turn up. When he got there today though he'd been assigned to a new Claims Officer.

"Suits me... Wagon!" he spat the words at the window.

"I'm sorry?" said Mona, looking a bit concerned.

"Oh no, not you! Sorry did I say that out loud? Sorry, having a bad day."

"You know you shouldn't call your girlfriend names like that!"

Ruarí burst out laughing at the thought of the cranky mare, with horrible glasses, in the dole office being his girlfriend. "No!" he was still laughing. "She's not my girlfriend. Just having a tough time finding a job and the dole office are giving me a hard time."

"Oh, I'm sorry about that love. I'll say a prayer for you."

"Thanks," said Ruarí out loud, and carefully under his breath added "for nothing!" before going back to watching the world go by out the window. He glanced at Mona a minute later and was surprised to see her, head down, hands clasped, eyes closed and her lips moving very slightly. His eyes darted back to the passing scene outside but he couldn't help looking at her again.

Suddenly he realised his stop was next so he reached across her to ring the bell.

She was smiling when she opened her eyes. "This is me." she said.

"Let me help you with those," said Ruarí. Despite his best efforts he just couldn't help liking her.

They got off the bus and he knew where to go but felt he had to pretend he didn't.

"Where to?"

"Oh, just up this way."

They were at his place now and just as he was about to ask for the next direction Mona pointed at the steps up to his bedsit and said, "Up you go!"

"How do you know I live here?" he smiled.

"Sure I've seen you every day since you moved in."

He went to hand her the shopping and she said, "No Ruarí, the shopping is for you."

"What? No! And how do you know my name?" He was laughing again. *'This woman is amazing!'* he thought to himself.

"Don't you worry about that. I was told you needed help and here's your help! Now off you go before the Fat Frogs defrost. Although I don't know how you eat those awful things."

Mona was already halfway across the road and Ruarí was still stood with his mouth open, thinking *'I LOVE Fat Frogs...'*

He let himself in and started to unpack the bags. All his favourite foods were there. Fat Frogs, corned beef –

not out of a tin, but thinly sliced from the deli counter, orange juice, and brown bread. Even shower gel! He'd run out and was using fairy liquid – he hated that. Four bags of groceries, every item he would have picked himself.

He wanted to run across the road to thank her and hug her and invite her for some corned beef sandwiches on brown bread, but he just sat slowly shaking his head, looking at all the stuff on the table.

* * * * *

The next morning Mona looked out the window and could see Ruarí crossing the road towards her house.

"Carole," she shouted up the stairs.

"Yes, Mam?"

"He's coming."

"OK, I'll stay up here 'til he's gone."

"Ah Carole come on! Are you not going to tell him? You have to tell him."

"No, Mam, I don't want to. Don't say anything. Not 'til after tomorrow anyway… Answer the DOOR will you?!"

Carole sat at the top of the stairs while Ruarí and Mona talked and laughed at the door. She looked down at the receipt in her hand. It was dated more than a month ago and was obviously for a shopping trolley filled with stuff for a single man. She smiled as she heard her mam keep her promise not to say how she knew what he needed. Mona made some excuse that she couldn't invite him in for a cup of tea, but maybe he'd come for a corned beef sandwich tomorrow. They laughed again as Carole went back into her room to finish packing.

She smiled and sighed. He had a face like thunder when he shoved that receipt, alongside the rest of the contents from his pocket, at her – but she couldn't say she blamed him.

At least now, before she left for Sydney, she knew she had been able to look after him in some way, and in turn he would look after her precious mother. Who would have thought she'd find someone else who loved corned beef sandwiches on brown bread? Her mam would delight in having someone else to make them for when she was gone too.

Carole tried to smile as she swallowed the lump in her throat and closed her suitcase. It was time.

The Disappearance Of
Bernie Francis

BERNIE Francis was a bully. She was what old Mrs Doherty called "a bitch in her heart." There was nobody safe from Bernie's smart comments or the flick of her hand as she passed you by. She was the talk of the town, but not for any good reason. Anyone who saw her coming the other way had to make a split second decision; '*Do I cross, or do I just let it happen; let her pass me and take what's coming?*'

She had a circle; you couldn't call them a circle of friends, but they were a circle alright. They gathered around her, protected her, lied for her, took the blame for her, and even took a few beatings for her.

She was untouchable, she was conniving, she was terrifying… and she was my sister.

Bernie and I didn't get on. We didn't spend any time together and thank God, since our older brother moved out, we didn't have to share a bedroom. We'd spend a few minutes at the breakfast table every so often and most days we all had dinner together, but only because my dad insisted. We never had anything to say to each other.

We moved in totally different worlds. I didn't want to have anything to do with her mates, and the only reason I never got a beating from them is because she was my sister. Though if they'd checked with her, they'd probably have found she wouldn't have minded. My friends escaped their wrath as well, which is probably the only reason I had any.

I don't know what made Bernie so angry. I asked her one day, why she hated everyone so much. She just pushed me. She couldn't stand the thought of anyone being happy. I actually believe it brought her pain. If she saw someone succeed or even buy something they'd saved for… as soon as she saw joy in their face she was unsettled and only felt relief if she found a way to ruin it.

She was vindictive, spiteful and very, very good at it.

When we went to visit Granny with mam and dad she'd be so nice. Not a peep out of her. "Please" and "thank you" for everything, but she knew what she was doing. Granny was always good for a few quid but you had to work for it; and Bernie always earned her money.

The worst thing she ever did almost had the police at the door. She was walking home from school with two of her gang and they saw Molly O'Brien coming towards them. We never really understood what was wrong with Molly. She had some sort of mild special needs, or a learning difficulty. The story goes that Bernie and two of her circle were coming through the park. Molly was coming towards them and she was singing but they dragged her up on to the bridge and made her sing louder. Up to that point most people felt it was typical of what Bernie would do; but then they stripped her naked and made her sing again. Rumour has it that Bernie tried to throw Molly off the bridge and into the shallow waters below, but one of her mates stopped her. So she just threw her clothes in the river and they ran off laughing.

Molly's parents came banging on our door the next day. There was a huge row, talk of the police and criminal prosecution. After they'd left, my dad threatened to send Bernie to a mental institution to have her head checked. There was a week or two of nervousness when I think even Bernie was on edge and my mam jumped every time the doorbell rang; but nothing came of it.

Someone once told me that they heard my dad went looking for Bernie in the park when she went AWOL not long after that. It was a regular haunt of hers and they had a blazing row when he went to hit her, but she hit him first. There was no evidence of this at home, but it wouldn't have surprised me. Bernie was definitely different after that though. I wonder if she knew she'd crossed a line and she'd seen in herself the depths that she could go to. How horrible, mean and deceitful she could be. When you care so little about people, do you eventually get an insight into your own badness? She'd gone beyond bully and I think she knew it.

We hardly ever saw her in the following weeks. She never ate with us. She'd go out early and come in late. There was nothing my mam or dad could do to change her. She refused to obey one rule. If they said to make her bed she'd mess it up worse. If mam said it was cold and she should close her coat, she'd take it off. She never did one scrap of homework and there were notes from teachers and letters from the school – but she didn't care. Mam and dad had meetings with the principal and there was talk of counselling and psychologists, but she wouldn't even speak to them. I heard mam crying to dad one night, saying how they were losing her. She was slipping away from them and there was nothing they could do to get her back.

Bernie got quieter and more distant. The odd time I passed her on the stairs, I noticed that her cruel attitude was changing. The look on her face was more despair and emptiness. She'd stopped hitting me as she passed me, so one day I got a bit brave and said to her, "You look like death Bernie." I thought she was going to push me down the stairs but she just looked back at me and said, "You'd love that wouldn't you? Da's pet. Well maybe you'll get your wish." And she kept walking. Maybe I should have known at that stage. I don't know why I didn't cop it, but I didn't.

Those were the last words we spoke to each other.

It was unusual, but not unheard of for her to stay out overnight, though it happened more and more. There'd be strained silences at breakfast as she came through the door and went straight upstairs. It slowly got worse, but we ignored it. "Least said soonest mended," had long been a mantra of my mother's, but that philosophy started to eat away at the heart of our family. Bernie had left us long before she stopped coming home.

When two weeks passed without any sign of her, mam's mantra was losing its hold over her. "Where is she? Why won't she come home? Is she dead John. God is she dead?"

Dad would just shake his head. Mam would try to hide tears, leaving the room to get something she didn't need. I'd just about be able to hear dad growl, "I'll kill that bitch when I get my hands on her." He was convinced she was slipping in and slipping out again without us knowing, but mam would have known. If a breath was taken in a room or the curtains moved a nanometre, she'd notice.

Dad finally got her to agree to let the police get involved. They gave up believing that she would just walk in the door. Getting the police in meant it was real and mam just could not handle that. They did searches, canvassed friends and neighbours, put up posters and set up a social media campaign. They even searched the Dublin Mountains. They didn't tell us that, I only heard because a friend of mine has a brother who is a detective and he had told her in confidence.

Every day the same thing: "Any news?" Mam would ask me and dad each time we walked into the room. When the phone rang she would run to it and instead of her signature cheery hello, she'd answer it with "Bernie, is that you love?"

My brother called in regularly, mainly to take some of the strain off dad. He'd listen to mam's stream of excuses and theories. Dad would go out to the shed or go for a walk to the park just in case. My brother would take him for a pint and mam would sit looking out the window.

Who would have thought that somebody's absence would take up so much space in a house? The things that drove us mad about her suddenly became funny and endearing. It was as if everyone had forgotten what a pain in the arse she was. For years Bernie had been a drain on the resources of our family; financially yes, but more so emotionally. Her disappearance didn't do much to reduce that, in fact it made it worse. Her presence had been exhausting, now her absence was paralysing.

The longer she was gone, the less I existed in my mother's eyes too. My presence was no comfort to her and eventually she stopped hiding her disappointment when it was me who came through the door. She would look past me, just in case Bernie was miraculously behind me.

The first Christmas Bernie was gone, mam bought and wrapped a big present for her and put it under the tree; she told everyone that Bernie would come home for Christmas. My brother and I got some cash in a card that had my dad's scribbled writing on it. My dad never wrote Christmas cards. Bernie was the only acceptable topic of conversation. My college work, my boyfriends, my new job, my new car – nothing was of interest to her and it took me a while to realise what was happening; I was disappearing too.

I lived at home longer than I wanted to; I didn't want to leave my dad there alone, but eventually I couldn't stand it anymore and got myself a flat that was a short walk from my parents' house. I wanted to be able to pop in regularly and for my dad to have somewhere he could go for respite. He came almost every day when I moved in first. He decorated every room and put up shelves and photos for me. He very often stayed for dinner and on occasion would sleep on my little sofa. "I just need a Bernie-free zone love!" he'd say.

*****

My mother's illness was short. She was sure she was dying of a broken heart, but it was aggressive and untreatable Breast Cancer. She told all the nurses, doctors and fellow patients about Bernie and was sure that if she knew how ill her mother was she'd come straight home.

As me and my father and brother sat by her bedside on her last night, we listened to her whimper. She never took my hand, or called my father to her. Bernie's name wasn't just her last word, it was her last fifty words.

When the doctor confirmed that mam had passed away, my brother walked out of the ward and my Dad turned to me with a combined look of pain and relief.

"Is she really gone? I can't believe it, is she really gone?"

"Yes, Dad," I said. "Bernie's gone."

Never Judge A Monk
By His Plumber

DOUGIE savoured the last few drags of his cigarette. It was the only downside to his regular trip to the monastery, absolutely no smoking in or outside the building. On the upside, he'd be very well fed today; nothing fancy but well-prepared meals, most of the ingredients homegrown. More often than not he'd leave with armfuls of fresh produce too. Dougie had been a self-employed plumber for more than 20 years. The regular answer to his wife's enquiry about his day was, "seen one radiator you've seen 'em all honey." But he always came home from the monastery with a story to tell.

Today was his quarterly visit to check the heating, plumbing and do any other odd jobs that were required. The Brothers would make a list between visits and Dougie would spend the day fixing, mending, painting – whatever needed doing. Landing the monastery contract was a gift. Though he knew old Brother Francis, in his Australian accent would have said "a blissing." Brother Francis was the eldest and, Dougie thought, the nicest of all the Brothers. He was a cheerful, gracious soul. He would bring Dougie drinks, ask about his family and make sure he left with plenty of homemade jam. If Dougie mentioned someone who'd been ill or had problems, Brother Francis would always remember the details. He'd have been praying fervently for that person and would check with Dougie how things were the next time he came.

Dougie drove up the lane that connected the back of the monastery's land to the road near his house. It was a handy shortcut that he only found by accident. As was often the case, the first sight that greeted him, apart from the monastery itself, was a washing line. On most occasions it was full of either bed linen or dark brown habits. It occurred to him once that he had never seen any underwear on the washing line. He mentioned this to his wife and with a deadpan expression she replied, "They must dry their smalls in private." Dougie almost choked on his dinner, spitting potatoes and peas everywhere. He still laughed at the thought of it and hoped one day to happen upon what they'd labeled 'the small private room' – but he never did.

When Dougie stopped for lunch Brother Francis joined him. They sat in the sun enjoying its warmth, and that of the breeze, as they chatted about many things; and it always surprised Dougie how much Francis knew of what was going on in the world. He analysed current affairs through the lens of his religious beliefs and seemed to have a story from the Bible that connected with every story in the newspapers. Dougie would never admit it, but he had no belief at all in what Brother Francis had to say. He was afraid of offending him, but more afraid that Francis might dislike him or disapprove of him as he, obviously, took his faith very seriously.

When they had finished their lunch, Brother Francis asked if he could add something to Dougie's job list. One of the legs on the chair in his room was coming loose; he had just noticed that morning and hadn't put it on the list. Dougie was more than happy to oblige and Brother Francis winked and promised an extra pot of jam to take home.

It was almost the end of the day when Dougie remembered the extra job. There was no one around, he reckoned they were probably at prayers before dinner, so he let himself into Brother Francis' room. He found the rickety chair and went to work, but eager to get on the road home he was hurrying and caught his finger with the pliers. He let a roar, using words that were probably never heard in that room before, jumped and knocked the books off Brother Francis' bedside locker. Faded photographs spilled out across the floor. As he picked them up he couldn't help but flick through them and thought he recognised Brother Francis in one or two, but he wasn't sure. The photos were a mix of old and new; families, couples, some children and one or two of scenic spots. Then he spotted the one that shocked him. It was a photo of a group of men on a beach, all in little swimming trunks. They were toned and tanned, with long shaggy blonde hair, each holding a surfboard. Dougie was stunned to find such a photograph in Brother Francis' possession and wasn't sure what to do next.

"They remind me to pray." Brother Francis was standing at the door. "They are all family and friends and at my age I need something to help me remember who I need to pray for."

Dougie wanted to disappear. "I am so sorry, I just… I hurt my hand and… they just… I knocked against your locker and… I'm really, really sorry."

"It's fine Dougie. Don't be troubled, there is nothing private in here. I have no sacred possessions. Anything sacred I have is inside me."

Brother Francis' warm smile allowed Dougie to relax and he was amazed at the humble spirit of this old man. He went to put the photos back when Francis took the one of the surfers from the top of the pile.

"You pray for surfers too then?" Dougie felt a little awkward.

"Oh, these are old friends. I doubt any of them surf now, but yes I still pray for them. And this photo comes in handy for something else too." Brother Francis gave one of his mischievous smiles.

"Oh yes?"

"Yes, it also reminds me to pray for myself."

Lovers

ACROSS the park he could see them, sitting in the glow of the moonlight. They seemed so connected, as if they never wanted to be apart.

He watched them silently court each other and imagined the sweet nothings they were hoping to communicate with just a look.

He carefully moved closer to them, to catch some of their conversation.

It was banal. They were holding back, hiding what they really felt.

In fact it was tantamount to lying, and lies made him feel really uncomfortable.

He took aim and pointed at the man – right at his heart.

Then he moved slightly so that he was now aiming at the woman's.

He couldn't decide who to shoot at first.

He knew he was a good shot and could shoot, reload and shoot again before either of them knew what was really happening, so he wasn't afraid of messing this up.

They didn't even hear the whip of the wind as the arrows headed towards them.

Suddenly the man felt a pain, like his heart was on fire – he'd never felt anything like it before and with a sharp intake of breath he looked at her and said, "I love you."

Then she felt it. "I know! And I love you too."

As they kissed, the shooter wiped the sweat from his forehead and smiled.

Then Cupid flew away to find his next target, thinking *'I love my job.'*

Moving The Threshold

SEBASTIAN looked around the living room with satisfaction. Everything was finally unpacked. It had taken time, but it was done. He loved his new apartment.

A little kitchenette opened out into a dining room area, which opened out a little wider to a living room. There was a small couch and a desk as well as a few books on the shelves, but no paintings on the wall and no photographs – and there wouldn't be. There were two bedrooms, the second of which he was using for storage. The only thing he wasn't sure about was the back garden area. The apartment block was slightly off the beaten track, safely tucked behind a tree-lined gated entrance. French windows at the back opened out to the garden; and it was beautiful. Glossy shrubs lined the wall and there was a burst of coloured flowers every four, or so, feet. The grass and borders were obviously regularly groomed. It was absolutely pristine.

It was perfect – well almost.

Immediately outside his French windows was an open-plan grass area shared by all the ground floor residents. There were no walls or fences, no lines of demarcation to state where his space ended and the neighbours' began.

Sebastian didn't like that. He preferred to know where the boundaries lay.

He had drawn an imaginary border in his head the day he viewed the apartment and discreetly asked the agent about it, but the original tenancy agreement had a 'communal area' clause. This had almost caused him to reconsider taking it; but everything else about it was so perfect.

The next morning he was sitting at his desk and could hear children laughing and calling to each other. He stood a few feet from the window and watched them. Two boys kicked a ball past his door. There was an ugly plastic slide with a little girl plodding her way up three clunky steps and sliding down the less than 18 inches to the ground, squealing with excitement.

Sebastian was not happy.

They obviously had no concept of the boundary, the slide definitely crossed it and one of the makeshift goal-posts was right outside his door. He wondered if may-be he should call the estate agent and tell them he had changed his mind. While he was pondering he heard tapping on the French windows. The little girl who had been on the slide was knocking and waving. Sebastian could not help but be charmed by her young enthusiastic innocence and opened the door.

"Hello Mr, Mummy said would you like a drink?"

"Excuse me?"

A woman appeared behind her.

"No, Jaden sweetheart, mummy said to ask if he liked to drink coffee. I'm sorry, my name is Skye. I live next door, wanted to welcome you and invite you in for coffee."

She was in her thirties, unkempt hair and stains on her clothes, but she had the brightest white cheery smile he'd ever seen.

"Eh, I usually only drink the one cup of coffee a day and I've had it, so maybe another time."

Sebastian closed the door firmly but as he was closing it he heard Skye say, "OK, goodbye, let me know if you need anything."

The following day an hour earlier, the little girl was at the door again. Sebastian was once again charmed by the cute smile, and noticed she was in the same grubby dress. He went and got his keys, picked up a sachet of his caffeine-free natural coffee substitute, closed all the win-dows and locked the back door.

He struggled to hide his shock as he stepped into Skye's apartment. The place looked like an explosion in a toy factory. There was stuff everywhere. No chair escaped without clothes or toys on it. Books, school bags, footballs, bicycles, dolls and prams were strewn everywhere.

"You'll have to take me as you find me I'm afraid. Here, let me clear a space for you to sit."

Sebastian didn't know where to look and immediately wanted to go back to the calm, quiet, cleanliness of his own house, but he didn't.

As usual he felt awkward conversing, but Skye chatted away and very soon he began to feel at ease. The life and excited purpose in Skye was beginning to have an effect on him. She had such enthusiasm as a mother; such freedom and enjoyment of her kids.

Sebastian had only ever received coldness from his mother. An insistence of quiet and the highest standard of cleanliness at all times. There was mayhem in this house, but it was beautiful. There was madness, disarray and disorganisation, but love!

There were no prying questions from Skye about his disability. She may have missed his pronounced limp, given the short distance between their apartments, but there was no way she'd have missed the disfigurement in his face or the speech impediment – yet she didn't make any reference to it and for the first time in his 57 years Sebastian felt accepted. He had spent his life separating himself from everyone – closing off the area around him, so that all that existed was his own small world. He was always repulsed when he caught sight of himself in a mirror but it suddenly occurred to him that not everyone saw what he saw.

He had allowed himself to forget interaction, community, neighbourhood and fellowship but Skye was reminding him what it was like to share coffee, time, friendship and even some germs!

He began to get nervous, worrying that he might outstay his welcome and he really did not want to do that. If he did, then maybe he would not be welcome again. He wanted to stay but for that reason he felt he had to leave and made his excuses. He thanked Skye for her hospitality and as he went to move felt something grab his knees. He looked down to see Jaden hugging his legs. "Goodbye 'bastian."

Sebastian tried to speak but couldn't, nor could he swallow.

The next day as he sat down to work he felt his apartment was too bare and quiet and so he did something completely out of character for him. He opened the door so he could hear the children play. Jaden was on the slide and when she saw him she let go to wave and almost fell. Sebastian jumped forward and caught her. "I nearly fell off the slide 'bastian." Her eyes were wide with fright.

"I know, you must be careful and hold on tight." He had gotten a fright too and sat her back up at the top of the slide. When he was sure she was OK he let go and she laughed as she slid to the ground.

Sebastian marvelled at her and her ability to find her way back to the top every time she found herself at the bottom; and he smiled as he realised, he could really learn something from this kid.

Girl Power

NANCY squirmed. She could see the 'Stella Girls,' as they were called, all hanging out of the school railings; shouting across the road at Terence Dunne. Poor Terence did his best to dodge the verbal stones. As he passed her, Terence gave Nancy a 'best of luck' glance and hurried on. Nancy barely had time for a 'thank you' grimace, he was gone. She decided to do what her brother Jason told her to do. Keep looking forward and keep walking. She was just glad that they were on the other side of the road.

As she got closer the stones started to fly again. "Ah look, it's Nancy Fancy Pants."

They'd called her that ever since the Scoliosis test day over a year ago. Nancy's mam had made her wear her Sunday pants. They were flowery and the only ones that didn't have a frayed hem or a hole in them. As each girl moved up the queue, the cold fact that they would have to strip down to their pants *before* going in behind the screen made them shiver. "You have to be ready for the doctor girls." Sister Majella had told them very kindly, as she tried to help each half-dressed girl hide from the rest. All the girls loved Sister Majella. Some loved her because she was kind, others because she was a pushover.

Standing in the queue Nancy thought, '*Thank God it's not Sister Bernadine!*'

Sister Bernadine would have had them all "ready for the doctor" as they stood in line!

Stories of Sister Bernadine's punishments were legendary and the threat of telling tales to her was more than enough to silence a classroom or end an argument. Nancy once heard that she caught someone cheating in an Irish test and they got 10 smacks with the ruler on their hand and then had no lunch. The girl whose work was copied got five days of detention for letting it happen too – even though she didn't know. When both girls' parents were called to the school Sister Bernadine shouted at them like they were kids themselves. No one knew who that happened to, but it didn't matter, everyone knew it was true.

So Sister Majella was indeed one of the few consolations of Scoliosis test day, but her presence was not powerful enough to stop Stella. Nancy was undressing just as Stella was joining the queue. "Ohh look at Nancy's pants. Nancy's fancy pants!"

Stella's gang loved the opportunity to support another one of her nasty campaigns and as Nancy stood there, for what felt like a week, she was jeered and mocked by the whole queue. Sister Majella tried to stop them, but no one wanted to be the person who went against Stella. It could make for a painful, or at the very least, uncomfortable lunch break.

Nancy did her best to keep her head up as she tried to ignore the memory of that awful day.

Her mam had asked her to get some shopping on her way home from school; so as well as her school bag she was also carrying heavy shopping bags. She couldn't swing her arms in that confident way that her brother had showed her, so she just kept walking.

Stella crossed the road and stood waiting for her.

"Hello, Nancy. Got your fancy pants on today?"

Nancy tried to get around her, but she was quick and moved to get in her way.

"Show us your pants Nancy, go on."

The Stella Girls were laughing and shouting across the road. Nancy tried to get around her again but Stella was always there first.

"Gowan, show us. Or maybe you don't have any on. I heard that you only have one pair and your ma doesn't even wash them properly."

Nancy went blind for a second. The mention of her mother sent red-hot flames through her body. She forgot she was even carrying stuff and with a rage that she had never felt before she took a swing at Stella. Stella didn't even see it coming – she was looking at her girls to make sure they were all laughing, but they'd stopped. It happened in a split second. "DON'T YOU EVER TALK ABOUT MY MAM!" Nancy screamed, like a banshee on Halloween night. Stella hit the ground and found herself looking at the sky. Pen, pencil, ruler, potatoes, carrots and a cauliflower went up in the air and rolled out on to the road. Nancy stood there breathing deeply as fire burned inside her.

She glared at Stella and was not afraid. Not anymore.

It didn't matter anyway, Stella was lying on the ground and to Nancy she just looked small.

"OK, OK," said Stella, slowly picking herself up.

The girls were silent as Nancy went out onto the road picking up the veg and her school stuff, putting it back into the bags.

Stella crossed the road and with false confidence said, "You think you're great don't you? Well I'm telling… my ma on you. You're going to be in trouble for this." Stella scowled at her girls who still had their mouths open, but her glare shook them back to submission as they tried to outdo each other by agreeing with her.

Nancy stared at them until they went quiet again.

"I don't care. Do you hear me?" Nancy got louder. "I don't CARE!!! Don't you ever say a word about my mam again. And don't ever call me names again. And just LEAVE ME ALONE. LEAVE PEOPLE ALONE AND DON'T BE SO HORRIBLE TO EVERYONE ALL… THE… TIME!!!"

"Nancy Cawley!"

They froze at the unmistakable voice of Sister Bernadine. "Stop that shouting and get in off the road!"

Stella and her girls looked at each other and one by one started to walk away, leaving Nancy to face Sister Bernadine.

When the Stella girls were finally out of sight though, Sister Bernadine did something Nancy had never seen her do before, and she smiled.

"Are you OK Nancy?"

"Yes, thank you Sister Bernadine."

Then she smiled again and Nancy could have sworn there was a glint in her eye as she said, "Good girl Nancy. Good girl yourself."

A Date With The
Domino Effect

SALLY let him hold the chair for her, slightly embarrassed. It wasn't something she was used to or particularly liked, but it was a special evening and she'd decided to go with the flow. She had spent ages deciding whether to be on time or to be early; fashionably late was another option. In the end she decided to be early as she wanted to be seated when he arrived – so she could avoid an awkward 'seating' moment, ironically. She chuckled.

"Everything OK madam?" The waiter was nodding and smiling a bit too enthusiastically for her liking, but she supposed it had looked like she'd laughed at him, so she cut him some slack.

"Yes, thank you."

"Anything to drink while you wait?"

"Yes, I'll have a glass of iced water, please."

Sally would have loved a glass of wine but didn't want him to arrive and find her drinking alone. What if he was late and found her with an empty glass in front of her? No, she'd decided to drink water until he arrived. All this had been thought out in advance and she was ready.

When Nick asked her out she was stunned. Sally wasn't the type to be self-deprecating, but she also wasn't the type to be asked out by the most popular guy at work. She'd known him for a couple of years, worked in his department for about five months and always thought he was too smooth to be silk. But in the last six weeks they'd been working on the same project.

It turned out to be far more enjoyable than she'd expected. Not just because he was fun to work with, but because he loved his work. He was a clever designer, saw things in a different way and was able to pitch things for the appropriate market without being sexist, ageist or anti/pro anything. It was a rare quality in designers and most who had it knew it, but it made them unbearable to be around. Not Nick, as it turned out.

When the project was in the wrapping-up stage he suggested they should meet up, but nothing came of that. Then on the launch day he asked her out for dinner and now here she was; as dolled up as she felt confident to be, sipping her iced water, waiting…

*

Nick walked to the bar and sat down just in time to see Sally being led to her seat. He was sorry now that he didn't call out to her when he saw her; instead he let her go in to the restaurant ahead of him. It was a silly mistake, but one that revealed to him just how nervous he was. He'd been a bit thrown that she insisted whoever got there first was to get the table, to save either of them waiting around at the bar. He'd got there a bit early so he could be there when she arrived but she'd obviously had the same idea. When he saw her getting out of her taxi just as he got out of his, he opened his mouth to call her name – but bottled it.

He was a bit jealous that the waiter got to hold the chair out for her. He'd have loved to do that. Now he was stuck at the bar with a drink. He couldn't stand there empty-handed so when the barman asked him if he wanted anything, he ordered a beer. He had to finish the drink before he sat with her; what would it look like if he got a drink before he'd even sat down?! Way too eager to get boozy, that's what!

He looked at her again and still couldn't believe she had said yes. Everyone said that Sally was a ball-breaker. Don Matheson was convinced she was batting for the other team but Nick knew that that stemmed from his failed attempt to kiss her at the Chairman's retirement do. Don didn't take rejection well.

Nick was so annoyed when his boss had paired him with Sally for the project. She was a far less experienced designer and he didn't have time for learners. But, as it turned out, she had an eye for detail that he hadn't seen in years. She was old school, in the best way. She understood the concept of a brand but didn't resort to stereotypes.

The day she added the tiny element to a storyboard that changed the whole thing and made the concept come alive, he'd almost grabbed her and kissed her. Instead though, he suggested they go for coffee but that conversation was interrupted by their boss coming in looking for an update. At the launch he asked her out to dinner, fully expecting a 'no', but here he was, he just needed to finish up his beer and go over to her.

He knocked back the last of the drink and as he did it occurred to him that now he was going to have a smell of alcohol on his breath when he met her. Already this date was going badly and he hadn't even said hello. He asked the barman where he could get breath-mints and was told that there was a vending machine in the lobby, so Nick slipped away.

*

It was only when he stood up that Sally realised the guy at the bar was Nick. She'd seen him nervously knocking back a beer and thought it could be him, but some lights and a complicated display on the bar obscured him. He did glance her way a couple of times though and when he stood up and moved she was finally sure it was him. She got her smile ready and actually felt a flutter of excitement as he started to walk across the restaurant; then the flutter fell and landed with a thump in the pit of her stomach as he disappeared around the corner.

'*He's leaving?!*' Sally thought she would cry. It was a combination of disappointment and anger. '*What was he doing standing at the bar drinking anyway?*' Sally didn't know what to do for a moment. Should she walk out, get that longed-for glass of wine or even order some food? She decided to wait. Maybe he was just gone to the bathroom. So she sat for a few moments trying to compose herself.

*

When Nick got to the vending machine he cursed the 'Out of Order' sign. He was going to go into the restaurant and take his chances but then he thought better of it. He'd spotted a late night pharmacy near the restaurant and was sure he could get something there – even if it was throat lozenges – anything to disguise the smell of the beer. He ran back through the lobby, out the door and down the street. Five minutes is all it would take and it would be worth it.

He didn't even see the two guys, standing at the corner of the side street, who followed him as he walked by.

*

Almost 20 minutes passed and Sally was now finished her water and ready to leave. She beckoned to the waiter and asked if it was possible that the man who'd been at the bar left a message for her. He went to check with the barman and on returning said that the man had ordered a beer, gone to the bathroom and then left the building. Sally thanked the waiter and asked for her coat.

Standing outside the restaurant she tried to hail a taxi.

114

About 100 yards up the road she noticed the flashing green cross of a late night pharmacy under which was a crowd of people, and two paramedics who were lifting a guy on to a stretcher.

Sally climbed into her taxi with a heavy heart and as it drove by the ambulance, the driver said, "I heard one of our guys calling for that ambulance on the radio. That guy was mugged by two yobos. This town is getting worse."

Sally saw a man with a bloodied nose being lifted into the ambulance. *'Poor guy,'* she thought. *'Shame it wasn't Nick! Now there's a guy who deserves a punch on the nose!'*

Suddenly Granny

DOLORES put the letter down and reached for her tea. It was stone cold. She looked up. She hadn't even clipped the top off the boiled egg.

"I need a mug of tea."

She put the kettle on and it started to quietly whistle and puff at her. She stared out the window. She had read the letter so many times she almost knew it by heart. It wasn't very long.

Dear Ma,

I don't know where to start. I suppose I better start by saying I'm sorry. I'm ok and I'm in London. I've been here for about two years…

"Two years? Where was she 'til then?" The kettle clicked. Dolores made the tea and sat back down at the table.

She picked up the letter and read it again.

You're not going to like this next bit. Even though I love it. I have a daughter. She's eight months old. Her name is Mia Dolores Ryan. So now you know. I'm not married either. Sorry.

"What kind of a name is Mia?! Mia Dolores. Mia… Dolores."

Mammy I want to come home. You probably don't want me to but I want Mia to grow up in Ireland. So I'm coming back. But I'll only come to Collinstown Park if you want me to. My flight is on the 27th of June.

"The 27th of June?" Dolores rooted in her bag for her diary. "Less than three weeks…"

I've written my number on the back. Will you ring me? It's an English number so you have to dial all the numbers. I'm really sorry Ma. I'd love to see you.

Love, Martina

PS: Mia sends a kiss to Granny.

Dolores put the letter down and sat back in the chair.

"Mia sends a kiss to Granny… Granny…" Hearing

herself say the words brought tears, then laughter, then more tears.

And while the tea went cold, Mia's Granny – she could get used to being called that – picked up the letter to read it again.

Remembering

ARTHUR bustled his way in through the door.

"I'm home Marge, I've made it! My goodness the shops are packed. You'd think it was Christmas Eve. Well all I want is a cup of tea. Would you like one love?"

Arthur put the kettle on and went through the bags of groceries, examining each item carefully before putting it away.

"And I'm having a couple of digestives! I know what you're going to say but I already worked them off getting on and off the bus... Oh no, I forgot the cheese."

Arthur opened the fridge to get the milk and there was the new block of cheese he'd just put there. He closed his eyes tightly and gently rocked back and forth trying to smooth the creases in his brain. The click of the kettle brought him back.

He brought the tea tray into the sitting room. As usual Marge's smile filled the whole room and immediately he was taken back to that first day and he could hear the music... *'If you were the only girl in the world and I was the only boy...'* It was his sister's wedding. Arthur had gone alone. Marge was there with some distant cousin called Frank. By the end of the night Frank was asleep in a corner and Marge was dancing with Arthur.

For a moment Arthur didn't know why Marge wasn't in her chair. He looked back at the photo of her – her smile never stopped making his heart swell. He spotted the knitting bag underneath her chair and suddenly felt very tired.

He sat down and went to pour the tea but just before pouring the second cup he was frozen in time. Why didn't it make sense?! It took a moment for him to reconcile the conflicting realities. Then looking at her photo once more he said, "I've done it again love," and he brought the second teacup back into the kitchen to put it back in the cupboard.

The Revolving Door

MARTY stood in his usual spot between the rubber plant and the security desk, with his back to the wall. Officially he was allowed to sit at the desk but standing gave him a better view of Marsha. She was one of a team of receptionists and though she worked different shifts, as luck would have it, she often worked when Marty was on duty. They worked in a large open-plan lobby, which consisted entirely of glass and marble surfaces. Even in bad weather it was a bright and cheery place to work, but never more than when Marsha was at her desk. For almost six months Marty had watched and listened to her.

"Good morning, *Bailey, Biscombe and Carlisle*, how can I help you?"

He had heard her say those words a thousand times and would have listened to her say them every day for the rest of his life, if he got the chance. Janice, Marsha's colleague, didn't answer the phone nearly as well; and as for Georgia – well she obviously hated her job. Georgia answered each call with a tone that matched her usually foul mood. Marty just knew that if he was ever in a position to invest money and rang Bailey, Biscombe and Carlisle, the sound of Marsha's voice would seal the deal.

He tried as best as he could to take his lunch break when Marsha did. She was usually on an early one but never ate in the canteen. Marty didn't mind, as long as she came back when he did. But a few folk were out sick that day and Marty's boss had radioed to say he'd have to take a later lunch as there'd be no one to relieve him for at least an hour, probably more.

Marty watched Marsha check the view from her little compact mirror, as she regularly did, before applying a fresh coat of her cherry pink lipstick and closing it with a satisfied snap. He listened to the sound of her heels as she gently clicked her way across the lobby, through the revolving door and out on to the street. He sighed a little, knowing that he'd probably be on lunch when she came back and that would mean two hours without seeing her. And to make matters worse, it was Friday. On Fridays she finished early and then he had the whole weekend to wait to see her again.

He was disturbed from his musing at the sound of her name.

"I'm going to miss Marsha." Janice had also watched Marsha leave.

"Really? Why? She's a bimbo."

Marty took a sharp breath and was about to defend Marsha's honour but thought, '*Hang on! Miss her? Where is she going?*'

"Ah, Georgia, she is not a bimbo. She's lovely and she's great to work with."

"Well I won't miss her. I hope her replacement has a better brain and a less squeaky voice."

Marty closed his eyes and held his breath. He wanted to walk over to Georgia and tell her to shut up, but he couldn't move. He felt a pain in his chest. He listened carefully, hoping to find out more about what was going on but a stream of phone calls distracted the receptionists.

When the phones quietened down again Georgia said, "Is the new girl starting straight away?"

"Yes, she's coming in on Monday. I'm doing a long day and she's going to shadow me."

"Great, you can have the newbie. I don't need the hassle." Georgia almost spat the words.

"You were a newbie yourself not that long ago." She was reminded.

"Yeah and I had Marshmallow Marsha training me in, is it any wonder it took me so long to get the hang of things?"

"Well I hope you signed the card at least. You coming to the goodbye drinkies tonight?"

Marty's eyes began to sting and his head hurt.

Marty? MARTY? MARTY DO YOU READ. OVER?

Marty's boss was growling through his radio.

"Sorry yes, Jacob. Over."

"Wake up will you? Ray is on his way down to take over from you, but grab a bite to eat and be back in a half hour. We're all on short breaks today. Over."

Marty handed over to Ray and went to the canteen. He ordered his usual Friday lunch, beef stew with a small bread roll but he hardly ate any of it. There was plenty of talk at the table about the match on Saturday while some chatted about that new movie, but he heard little and said nothing before hurrying back to his station.

Ray stood up from the desk, said something to Marty and headed off as Marty took his place by the rubber plant just in time to see Marsha return to her post.

All afternoon he savoured every call that Marsha answered and every so often he felt a lump in his throat that he had to swallow hard. As 4pm approached, Marsha's Friday finishing time, his heart sank lower and lower. Friday afternoons always went too fast, but this one was slipping away from him at a painful rate.

Just before four, there were hugs and handshakes as people came down from their offices to say goodbye. There were promises of a dance later, more hugs and even a few tears from Janice.

Eventually Marsha gathered all her stuff together and walked past Marty for the last time.

"Goodbye, Marsha, all the best."

The words were out of his mouth before he knew it.

Georgia and Janice looked up at him, then at each

other. Georgia snorted and picked up a call.

Marsha walked over to Marty.

"Nawwwwh, thanks. It's…. Martin isn't it?"

His heart leaped at the sound of her voice almost getting his name right.

"Ehh Marty, but… but you can call me Martin if you like."

Marsha giggled. "You're funny. I'm sorry I never got the chance to get to know you before I left."

"I'm sorry too."

He said it like he meant it and Marsha beamed.

"Would you like to come to my goodbye drinks thing? They're on in the Maybourne Hotel, you know on the corner? We're meeting about 6pm. But you'll have to change out of that uniform – although I do love a man in a uniform…" She giggled again.

He could hear Janice and Georgia laughing, but he didn't care.

"Eh yeah, no, yeah, I'd eh, yeah. I'd love to thanks."

"Greaaaaat! Well I'll see you later… Martin."

"And I'll see you later… Meesha."

Marsha giggled. "You're funny," she said again.

As he watched her walk across the lobby, Marty wondered why Georgia and Janice were both on the phone and people were just coming and going, in and out of offices. Didn't they notice that the world was a fantastic place to be? He sat down at the security desk. His feet were killing him and he was really hungry but he was also the happiest man in the world as Marsha stopped, gave him a little wave and a big smile before disappearing through that revolving door.

Who knows what would happen when they met the other side of it.

A Mallet In The Sales

MAURICE was very nervous. Twisting his fingers he tried to answer the question but his mind went blank.

"It's OK, Mr Mallet. Take your time. It's an interview, not an interrogation." The interviewer forced a smile.

"Well," he swallowed. "My area of sales is... selling encyclopaediae door to door."

"Mr Mallet! I'm sorry." The interviewer was stern again. "Your CV says you have been with the same company for the last 30 years and just finished in that position six weeks ago! No one has sold encyclopaediae door to door for at least 10 years."

"That's not true," said Maurice indignantly. "It's just that no one has BOUGHT one for 10 years!"

Lost And Found

DEE was frantic, throwing cushions off the sofa, rummaging in coat pockets, shaking shoes upside down. But it seemed the keys had gone – just disappeared. Frustrated she grabbed her hair and began to tug at it. A bad habit she'd formed over years of becoming more easily agitated. It never helped, it's not like it relaxed her; but it was like a tic now and she couldn't help it. She slumped on to the sofa. There would be trouble when Barry came to collect the kids. The deal was he would take them, and the car, for the day. That was the arrangement and Barry didn't like to be messed around.

She could hear the kids upstairs getting ready for their day out with dad. She always felt a bit jealous that they were looking forward to it so much. Then she'd feel guilty. She had to concede that even though he hadn't been the supportive, loving husband she needed, he was a great dad.

She went around the house again, every bag, every shelf, every pocket – the car keys were nowhere to be found. She knew Barry would accuse her of doing it deliberately and she really didn't want to fight, not today. She wondered if he would remember the date.

Upstairs she checked with the girls again but they didn't know. It wasn't unheard of for Hannah to take keys and put them in her dolls' house but Dee had checked and double-checked; and Hannah promised that she hadn't taken them. She went into Jennifer's room, where Jennifer was sitting on her beanbag playing with her phone, for another look.

"Are you ready for when your Dad comes and are you sure you haven't seen the keys?"

"Yes and yes," Jennifer replied rolling her eyes – her standard response these days.

Dee ran back downstairs and stood in the kitchen

holding her hair. She traced her steps again in her head. Getting back from the supermarket, letting herself into the house, then back and forth to bring in the bags. She definitely locked the car so they weren't there, but in desperation she went back out to have a look. While she was circling the car, peering in each window, Barry arrived on his motorcycle.

"Please do not tell me you've locked the keys in the car!"

"I wish I had, but no. Barry I'm sorry, but I can't find them. I'm after searching the house 10 times in the last hour. They have just disappeared."

"Don't Dee, don't start now. There's always something and…"

"There isn't always something and I'm not starting. Those girls are dying for their day out – do you think I'd do that to them?"

Barry slammed open the side gate of the house and locked his bike up.

"Come on, I'll help you look."

They went into the house and he called the girls. Hannah came running and Jennifer eventually followed, still texting.

"Hello, Jennifer, earth calling."

"Hi, Dad." She gave him an absent-minded kiss on the cheek and put the TV on.

"Don't start watching anything, we'll be going as soon as we find the keys."

Jennifer collapsed on to the sofa and started to flick through the stations while Barry went over the same ground that Dee had three times already.

An hour later Dee was at the kitchen table drinking tea. Barry was standing at the sink looking out the window and every so often he'd suggest somewhere they'd both looked twice already.

"Maybe we were all meant to be together today." Dee was tentative as she spoke.

"Why?"

"Don't you remember what today is?"

"Of course I remember. Why do you think we should spend it together this year? We never have before."

"That's right. You left me before the first anniversary." It was out before Dee could catch it. She closed her eyes and braced herself for Barry's retort – but though he bristled, he didn't respond.

He was still looking out the window when he said, "Matt and Sue's young fella joined the Little Kickers last week. He was telling me in the pub the other night. Was thinking that it would have been Ian's year to join too."

It was the first time Dee heard Barry say Ian's name since he'd walked out, not long after Ian had been taken away almost four years previously.

"And that's my fault too I suppose?"

"No, no. For God's sake Dee, I was just telling you. I know it wasn't your fault, no one is to blame. He just… he just died."

For a long time they were silent, both thinking back to when Hannah and Ian were born.

Dee hadn't realised she was expecting twins until Hannah was delivered and she remained in labour; 15 minutes later Ian arrived. Dee and Barry, who had tried for five years for another baby, couldn't believe their luck, it was a fabulous surprise to have twins. Jennifer was 10 and they'd almost given up hope of a second child; now they had three! For eight months everything was crazy, but fantastic. They could not have been happier. Then one morning Dee went to feed Ian, wondering why he wasn't already crying for his bottle. When she picked him up he was already cold. Paramedics tried everything but Dee knew the moment she had touched him that he was gone. Barry got really drunk the following day and came home shouting and crying for his son. He screamed at Dee, telling her it was her fault, and within a month he had moved out of the house. The first year had been terrible but slowly they began to make practical arrangements and were now able to be fairly civil to one another. Dee had many reasons to be angry with Barry, but he was a devoted father.

The sound of Hannah's voice brought them both back to the sadness of the present day, but also made them smile. "Mammy, I'm hungry."

Dee scooped her up and gave her the biggest cuddle. "Of course you are love. By now you and Jen and Dad should be having your lunch."

"Is Daddy having his lunch here?"

Dee turned to Barry, with Hannah still in her arms, and asked him the same question with her eyes.

"Only if I can have one of those cuddles that Mammy got."

Hannah's smile, 10 times cuter than usual with the missing tooth, melted both their hearts and for a split second things almost felt like they used to. Hannah held her arms out to Barry and he grabbed her and swung her around.

"Why don't you play with Daddy while I make lunch?"

Barry and Hannah were sat at the table playing cards while Dee prepared the food. Jennifer came into the kitchen. "Are we not going out Dad? I've spent ages getting ready and now we're staying in? And having lunch here? No McDonalds? What are you making Mum? I don't want a toasted sandwich. I'm going to my room." Jennifer stormed out of the kitchen and went upstairs.

"What was that about? I couldn't get a word in."

Barry shrugged and pretended to cry while surrendering some cards to Hannah. Hannah laughed and grabbed them out of his hands.

Upstairs Jennifer lay on her bed. She had been listening very carefully to her parents' conversation and enjoyed the feeling of the tension beginning to make way for peace. Her phone buzzed again, a text message from her friend Beth.

"Well?"

"Yep, he's staying for lunch."

"Wot will u do now?"

"Don't know, jus c how it goes?"

"OK have 2 go. Msg me l8tr?"

"Yea, will do. Tnks xxx"

"No probs. Luv you babe xxx"

"U 2 x"

The call for lunch came from downstairs and Jennifer shouted that she was coming; but not before she snapped her phone shut and slid her hand under her pillow… just double-checking the car keys were still there.

Artistic Temperament

THE picture on the wall opposite her was a good distraction and Orla wondered if it was there deliberately, to keep people calm. It was an abstract painting of a view of Paris. The Eiffel Tower was leaning almost like The Tower of Pisa and all the colours were strong with outlines that were childlike in their style; thick and crooked. But it was obviously a professional job. It was a fascinating image almost hypnotising Orla, helping her to forget how nervous she was.

"Orla Geraghty?"

She stood at the sound of her name.

"You can go in now."

She took a deep breath, and holding her portfolio tight in her hands she walked to the door. She then gave a confident knock and opened it when she heard the acknowledgement.

The room was bright and airy, a modern conference room with paintings on the wall obviously done by the same artist as the one out in the waiting room. Three people sat at chrome and black desks with their backs to the windows – all had pens and pads and on the table in front of them were bottles of water and bowls of mints. It reminded her of a cross between *Dragon's Den* and *The X Factor*.

There was no chair for Orla to sit on – just an easel on which to place her work. She was glad as she would be much happier standing. She strode across the room and leaned her portfolio against the easel with confidence, and a determination not to be all fingers and thumbs. The letter had said that her presentation was to have no technology and no fancy powerpoint presentations or time-consuming videos. Just her and her art – which suited her fine. Art was what she did best.

She turned to smile at the three interviewers. One was

a young woman, not much older than herself, who was dressed very stylishly and had an interesting headpiece that matched her outfit. In the middle was an older man in a suit that was obviously handmade. Orla reckoned he was probably one of those men who was nearing 60 but looked ten years younger. He was tanned and very attractive. The third interviewer was the eldest of the three. He was in a more functional suit, which probably fitted him a little better a year ago, and there was something about him…

As Orla scanned his face her smile faltered and a flash of recognition passed between them. The other two did not notice, when for a split second, they locked eyes, but then the moment passed.

Orla had to keep it together.

"Miss Geraghty, are you happy for me to call you Orla?" The woman spoke.

"Yes, please do."

"OK, I'm Genevieve Faulkner, Chief Designer on the project. Sylvio Matiz is our COO and Frank Dillon is a brand consultant. Orla, you know why you are here, so please show us what you have for us."

Orla smiled and nodded across the table before beginning her presentation.

For more than half an hour she displayed her work, as one by one she explained the concepts, materials used and connections to other commissions while working in connections to the project that the interview was all about. She smiled and spoke with enthusiasm as she talked about the love of her life, art.

She made regular eye contact with the first two interviewers and only glanced in the direction of the third every so often, so that it was not obvious she was avoiding further eye contact. He seemed to have picked a spot on the wall anyway and spent most of his time nodding and shifting uncomfortably in his chair.

It was clear, however, that the panel was impressed with her work and she left the interview torn between feeling confident that she did well and hoping that she never had to enter that building again.

Sitting in a café just a few minutes walk from the interview, she pondered both it, and interviewer number three. What were the odds that they would bump into each other again; and so soon? She had managed to hide her embarrassment when she saw him, and kept her game face on.

As she was thinking she didn't realise she was fiddling with the portfolio, which was leaning up against the window of the café. It was about to fall over when she grabbed it in time but almost knocked her coffee over in the process. When she gathered herself and looked up, he was standing in front of her.

"May I sit down, Orla?"

"I suppose so."

"I just wanted to say thank you, for not saying anything at the interview."

"You're welcome, I suppose. But you can imagine, it was a shock to see you there."

"Well I didn't expect to see you today either and, to be honest, my plan was not to see you ever again."

"Really? You didn't say that when you left last night. But if that is what you want, I understand."

He nodded gravely. "Well I'd better get back, I just wanted to say thank you for not saying anything. And… I… shouldn't tell you, but you'll probably get a phone call today – offering you the job."

"Are you serious? Oh wow, that's amazing. Fantastic!"

"So you're OK with seeing me again?"

"Of course. You're the one who is uncomfortable about last night, not me. And I presume you'll be fully clothed from now on?"

"Yes! That was my first and last time. Why I thought I could be a model for a life drawing class I have no idea!"

Friends Reunited